TOEFL
托福文法與構句

李英松／著

上冊

n't have a carefully developed plot. (主格補語) Whatever you decide will be fine

at red bicycle. (介詞的受詞) Do you know what happened

The painter gave whatever spots to the rest of my tuna fish sandwich

had another coat of enamel. (間接受詞) Roth mowed the

ha ed out the weeds, while we weeded

d not the roses. Give some consideration to those whoever you

hours in the hot sun had 形容詞子句——當做形容詞

us feel as though the day would never end.

ist of of people and some that contain is a group

language that we use during our childhood

立子句（或稱主要子句），可以單獨存在成為句

可以和另外一個獨立子句連結，The gymnasts and their

me 能完整表達意思。William read The Washington Post an

station. (句 Our class is writing stories for the second graders at Thomson Elementary Sch

e to subway station, and I arrived at school on time. (兩個

自序

　　托福考試的主要內容分為四大類—聽力、字彙、文法和閱讀。全部試題均有四個答案，除了文法類的試題有一半是選擇正確的答案，另外一半卻要選擇錯誤的答案之外，其餘聽力、字彙和閱讀都是要選擇正確的答案。

　　四大類的題目是非常多，應考者所能利用的時間平均每一道題不到十秒鐘。因此應考者一定要抓住時間，分秒必爭，否則時間是不夠用。

　　聽力類——在聽完一對男女談話的錄音帶之後，測驗應考者對於談話內容的了解程度。

　　字彙類——在　個或兩個句子當中挑出一個關鍵字，要應考者選出一個相似字或片語以便符合原來句子的意義。

　　文法類——雖然文法規則非常多，但是只要觀念正確，條理分明，應考者應該不難辨別一或兩句的英文當中，哪裡是正確或錯誤。

　　閱讀類——看完三或四篇短文之後，必須要認知文章的內容，它們的主題是在敘述什麼？換句話說，人、事、時、地和物在文章中的位置，那麼在答題的時候，可以不費吹灰之力就能夠找出答案。千萬要注意，試題紙上不可做任何記號，發揮自己大腦強大的記憶力，這時候可以充分的展現。

　　本冊（上冊）和中冊書均在分析托福考古題有關文法的部份，當應考者看完試題當下，就應該知道這個題目是要考我們什麼？迅速的在四個答案中選擇一個作答。要能達到這樣的功力，讀者務必要不斷的自我練習作答，最終可以領會一看試題就知答案的境界。

　　通過托福考試（一直都是以 500 分為標準），也順利的申請到學校的 I–20（入學許可證），來到要入學的學校註冊之後，在開學之前，學校還會再辦理一次托福考試，內容除了前面所提四大類之外，還有可能再加作文和面試。萬一沒有達到 500 分以上，選修課程時必需修兩個到六個學分的英文課，面對這種結局，不但浪費時間也損失不少金錢，有意留學的年輕讀者們加油啊！

目錄

第十八章 | 托福文法考古題解析

〈從四個答案當中，選擇一個正確的答案〉

1. The organizers of the convention have arranged accomodations for those
   participants_____ from out of town.
   （A）which will come
   （B）are coming
   （C）who comes
   （D）coming
   <解答> D（縮減的子句）

2. The playgrond supervisor reprimanded _____ for our shouting.
   （A）ourselves
   （B）us
   （C）ours
   （D）we
   <解答> B（代名詞形式）

3. The job applicant was worried about the interview_____ he was well
   prepared.
   （A）because
   （B）if
   （C）unless
   （D）even though
   <解答> D（連接詞形式）

4. The human rights activist considered it_____ honor to be nominated for the award.

（A）an

（B）a

（C）the

（D）this

＜解答＞ A（冠詞形式）

5. Although the members of the faculty seem inflexible, _____ to suggestions.

（A）they are always open

（B）always they are open

（C）open they are always

（D）they are open always

＜解答＞ A（字序）

6. Some consider Las Vegas_____ city in the world to live in.

（A）the bad

（B）worse

（C）worst

（D）the worst

＜解答＞ D（副詞比較）

7. The parent scolded the child and made her promise_____ again.

（A）never to do that

（B）what to do never

（C）that never to do that

（D）so never to do that

＜解答＞ A（名詞從屬子句）

8. Highly motivated, ambitious people often_____ more hours in a day.

（A）needing

（B）need

（C）needed

（D）are needing

＜解答＞ B（動詞時態）

9. An employment survey revealed today that demand for high-level excutives
   _____ increased this year.
   （A）have
   （B）be
   （C）has
   （D）were

   ＜解答＞ C（動詞一致性）

10. Every fall geese_____ over the house located directly on the bay.
    （A）fly
    （B）flies
    （C）have flown
    （D）flown

    ＜解答＞ A（動詞一致性）

11. The Rosetta stone has provided scientists_____ a link to ancient civilizations.
    （A）of
    （B）to
    （C）by
    （D）with

    ＜解答＞ D（介詞）

12. Carnival sideshows often feature acrobats who judge knives and balls_____
    same time.
    （A）all at the
    （B）at all
    （C）all at a
    （D）all at some

    ＜解答＞ A（冠詞）

13. _____ the railroads were built, early settlers had organized an elaborate
    system of trails and canals.
    （A）After

（B）During

（C）When

（D）Before

＜解答＞ D（副詞從屬子句）

14. National Park conservationists think_____ concession stands mar the natural beauty of the park.

（A）of

（B）about

（C）that

（D）a lot

＜解答＞ C（名詞從屬子句）

15. The grasslands and deciduous forest climates are similar except that the former receives_____ rainfall.

（A）least

（B）few

（C）less

（D）fewer

＜解答＞ C（比較）

16. _____ lunch, the finance committee resumed the meeting.

（A）Having to eat

（B）Have to eat

（C）Having eaten

（D）Having eat

＜解答＞ C（縮減的副詞從屬子句）

17. Powder when mixed with water_____.

（A）dissolving

（B）dissolves

（C）it dissolve

（D）dissolved

＜解答＞ B（動詞時態）

18. Water boils_____ if there is a cover on the pan.

　（A）faster

　（B）more fast

　（C）as fast as

　（D）fast

　＜解答＞ A（比較）

19. If there life on Mars, such life forms_____ unable to survive on earth.

　（A）would be

　（B）are

　（C）will be

　（D）should

　＜解答＞ A（條件句）

20. The damage was caused by either the earthquake_____ the subsequent explosions.

　（A）and

　（B）but

　（C）then

　（D）or

　＜解答＞ D（連接詞平行構句）

21. Fatal reactions to bee stings among adults_____ than once believed.

　（A）more are probably common

　（B）more common probably

　（C）are more probably common

　（D）are probably more common

　＜解答＞ D（字序）

22. Because of intermittent charging by the_____, the lights flickered.

　（A）generation

　（B）general

　（C）generator

　（D）generated

<解答>　C（易混淆的字）

23.　The static interference on the radio_____ an airplane.

（A）was caused by

（B）was causing

（C）has caused

（D）caused by

<解答>　A（被動語態）

24.　The management requests that all personnel_____their complaints to their immediate supervisor.

（A）will direct

（B）directs

（C）directing

（D）direct

<解答>　D（假設語態）

25.　Although we sent out invitations, we have no idea_____ coming to the party.

（A）who are

（B）whom are

（C）who is

（D）whom is

<解答>　C（主詞動詞一致性）

26.　The pioneers_____ the frontier had a difficult life with few comforts.

（A）on

（B）in

（C）inside

（D）over

<解答>　A（介詞）

27.　The typist was fast_____, and was hired immediately.

（A）but efficient

（B）and efficiently

（C）so efficient

（D）and efficient

<解答> D（連接詞平行構句）

28. The＿＿＿ economy at the turn of the century was due in large part to the influx of thousands of immigrants.

（A）rapid expanding

（B）rapid expand

（C）expand rapidly

（D）rapidly expanding

<解答> D（字序）

29. Mr. Kwok cooks continental cuisine＿＿＿ as the best cooks in Europe.

（A）as good

（B）as better

（C）better

（D）as well

<解答> D（比較）

30. Some doctors involved in brain research＿＿＿ that violence has its roots in certain sections of the brain.

（A）are believing

（B）believe

（C）believing

（D）believes

<解答> B（動詞時態）

31. Even＿＿＿ to believe otherwise, the central Arctic is not a solid sheet of ice.

（A）though many do not want

（B）many do want not

（C）though not many do want

（D）many do not want

<解答> A（副詞從屬子句）

32. After＿＿＿ the angry mob shouting for his resignation, the President summoned his loyal aides to his office.

（A）their hearing

（B）they hearing

（C）heard

（D）hearing

＜解答＞ D（縮減的副詞從屬子句）

33. The farmers recruited to work in the paper mill complained that they were not accustomed_____ a timecard.

（A）to punching

（B）to punch

（C）by punching

（D）having punched

＜解答＞ A（動詞片語）

34. _____ the lawyer's opinion, the case should not to trial.

（A）By

（B）On

（C）In

（D）With

＜解答＞ C（介詞）

35. _____ the predicament and solving it are two different problems.

（A）Indentification

（B）Identifying

（C）It is indentifying

（D）To identify

＜解答＞ B（連接詞平行構句）

36. The spectators breathed a sigh of relief when_____.

（A）the whistle has blown

（B）the referes blows the whistle

（C）they heard the final whistle

（D）the whistle blows

＜解答＞ C（動詞時態）

37.　　＿＿＿＿ rain now, the farmers will have to postpone the harvest.

　　（A）It should

　　（B）Will it

　　（C）Should it

　　（D）When it will

　　＜解答＞　C（倒裝句）

38.　　The phonograph next door was so loud that we could＿＿＿＿ hear the television in our own room.

　　（A）hard

　　（B）harder

　　（C）hardly

　　（D）hardy

　　＜解答＞　C（易混淆的字）

39.　　The motivation of the workers　　　　 not a monetary reward, but the satisfaction of a job well done.

　　（A）was

　　（B）were

　　（C）should be

　　（D）could be

　　＜解答＞　A（主詞動詞一致性）

40.　　Lawmakers are considering banning both beer＿＿＿＿ wine commercials from television.

　　（A）also

　　（B）than

　　（C）or

　　（D）and

　　＜解答＞　D（連接詞形式）

41.　　Of the many opinion expressed to the council members by the various citizens' groups present, ＿＿＿＿ was the only opinion that mattered.

　　（A）their

（B）their one

（C）theirs

（D）they

　　＜解答＞　C（代名詞形式）

42.　If poisons like DDT_____ to control insect, there will be serious
environmental repercussions.

（A）use

（B）uses

（C）are used

（D）used

　　＜解答＞　C（條件句）

43.　Literature_____ provides only fragments of information about the Anglo
Saxon period.

（A）recorded in the century tenth

（B）in the recorded tenth century

（C）in the century tenth recorded

（D）recorded in the tenth century

　　＜解答＞　D（字序）

44.　Technology has increased____, or the amount of goods and services
available.

（A）produce

（B）productivity

（C）producers

（D）products

　　＜解答＞　B　（易混淆的字家族）

45.　The receptionist, _____ job it was to answer the phone, had laryngistis.

（A）whose

（B）who

（C）who's

（D）that

<解答> A（形容詞從屬子句）

46. The embezzler, _____ his actions, wanted to make restitution to the company.

（A）were

（B）regretful

（C）was regretting

（D）regretting

<解答> D（縮減的形容詞子句）

47. _____ is thought to be one of the best investments of the decade.

（A）That the artist works

（B）That the artists work

（C）The work of that artist

（D）That the artists, work

<解答> C（主詞動詞一致性）

48. In one year rate eat 40 to 50 times_____ weight.

（A）its

（B）and

（C）their

（D）of

<解答> C（代名詞一致性）

49. Little is known about platinum_____ so little of it exists.

（A）but

（B）why

（C）because

（D）although

<解答> C（連接詞形式）

50. After_____ the supernova hurls its mass into the black void of space.

（A）it exploding

（B）exploding

（C）explosive

（D）explodes

<解答>　B（縮減的副詞從屬子句）

51.　The vineyards are open all year except for August, which＿＿＿＿.

（A）the best time to harvest is

（B）is the best time to harvest

（C）to harvest is the best time

（D）the best time is to harvest

<解答>　B（字序）

52.　New research in geophysics disproved＿＿＿＿ had been a universally accepted truth.

（A）that

（B）which

（C）whom

（D）what

<解答>　D（名詞從屬子句）

53.　Water vapor＿＿＿＿ on a window pane produces condensation.

（A）which accumulating

（B）accumulating

（C）accummulates

（D）is accumulating

<解答>　B（縮減的形容詞子句）

54.　The mayor felt that the police, in spite of the reports, had done＿＿＿＿ best in a difficult situation.

（A）is

（B）their

（C）his

（D）our

<解答>　B（代名詞一致性）

55.　＿＿＿＿ there is a snowstorm or some other bad weather, the mail always comes on time.

（A）Because

（B）If

（C）So

（D）Unless

＜解答＞ D（ 連接詞形式）

56. Since calculators were introduced, they＿＿＿ to be useful tools for people weak in math.

（A）proved

（B）will prove

（C）have proved

（D）are proving

＜解答＞ C（動詞時態）

57. Not being able to determine what＿＿＿ is the biggest obstacle for new managers.

（A）the priority should be

（B）it should be the priority

（C）should the priority be

（D）should be it the priority

＜解答＞ A（字序）

58. The nation was founded on the principle that all men are created＿＿＿.

（A）equitable

（B）equality

（C）equal

（D）equilibrium

＜解答＞ C（易混淆的字）

59. That woman＿＿＿ speaking softly can barely be understood.

（A）whose

（B）whom is

（C）who is

（D）who

＜解答＞ C（形容詞從屬子句）

60. The language of the Sumerians, _____ is unrelated to any known language.

    （A）which remains obescure origin

    （B）whose origin remains obscure

    （C）whose remains obscure origin

    （D）who is origin obscure remain

    ＜解答＞ B（形容詞從屬子句）

61. Although the mission was to be kept secret, it_____ to the press.

    （A）reveals

    （B）revealed

    （C）was revealed

    （D）reveal

    ＜解答＞ C（被動語態）

62. Foreign aid funds_____ by the committe at the President's recommendation.

    （A）were cut

    （B）will cut

    （C）cut

    （D）cut it

    ＜解答＞ A（被動語態）

63. The questions to the Board_____ in a belligerent tone by the stockholder.

    （A）poses

    （B）was posed

    （C）were posed

    （D）posed

    ＜解答＞ C（被動語態）

64. The commissioners assured the crowd that the problem_____ care of as soon as possible.

    （A）has been taken

    （B）had been taken

    （C）will take

    （D）will be taken

<解答> B（被動語態）

65. When the facade needed to be renovated, the building committee voted

to_____.

（A）havbe done it

（B）have it done

（C）be done

（D）have been done

<解答> B（被動語態）

66. _____ eagle is the national bird of the U. S. A.

（A）A

（B）An

（C）The

（D）0

<解答> C（冠詞）

67. The cat is_____ beautiful animal, but its intelligance leaves much to be

desired.

（A）a

（B）on

（C）the

（D）0

<解答> A（冠詞）

68. Families like_____ Rockefellers have become synonymous with wealth.

（A）a

（B）an

（C）the

（D）0

<解答> C（冠詞）

69. _____ University of Chicago has an excellent law school.

（A）A

（B）An

（C）The

（D）0

<解答> C（冠詞）

70. _____ Finland known for its beautiful forests and seacoasts.

（A）A

（B）An

（C）The

（D）0

<解答> D（無冠詞）

71. It took five men to carry the tree, which was_____ than a three-story building.

（A）taller

（B）as tall

（C）more taller

（D）the tallest

<解答> A（比較）

72. The plan to use existing resurces was considered the_____ solution.

（A）good

（B）most better

（C）best

（D）more better

<解答> C（比較）

73. The weather is_____ at this time of year than in the spring.

（A）calm

（B）calmest

（C）calmer

（D）more calmer

<解答> C（比較）

74. The appreciation of platinum is_____ subject than that of gold to the vagaries of international circumstances.

(A) less

(B) few

(C) fewer

(D) least

＜解答＞ A（比較）

75. Of all the amplifiers, this product with its wide range provides_____ stability within the audible spectrum.

(A) the greatest

(B) the greater

(C) greater

(D) greatest

＜解答＞ A（比較）

76. If they_____ overworked in the beginning, the volunteers would have helped finish the project.

(A) were not

(B) was not

(C) had not been

(D) have not been

＜解答＞ C（條件句）

77. The supervisors could have prevented this problem_____ it Beforehand.

(A) if they knew

(B) had they known

(C) if had they known

(D) whether

＜解答＞ B（條件句）

78. Because Mr. Gleason worked only a month, the personnel director would not write a recommendation for him even if he_____.

(A) could ask

(B) asks

(C) asked

（D）will ask

＜解答＞ C（條件句）

79. The teaching assistant's explanations to the class will be more understandable if he_____ more clearly next time.

（A）speaks

（B）spoke

（C）will speak

（D）has spoken

＜解答＞ A（條件句）

80. Had the damage been worse, the insurance company_____.

（A）would pay

（B）paid

（C）would have paid

（D）had paid

＜解答＞ C（條件句）

81. _____ the classroom needs to be cleaned.

（A）The offices and

（B）Either the offices or

（C）Both the offices

（D）The offices nor

＜解答＞ B（連接詞形式）

82. The baby_____ cries if he cannot get his way.

（A）screams but

（B）screams and

（C）screams neither

（D）either screams nor

＜解答＞ B（動詞一致性）

83. The group of students touring on bicycles went_____ to the mountains, but to the coast as well.

（A）either

（B）also

（C）neither

（D）not only

＜解答＞ D（連接詞形式）

84. The statesman gave us his reasons for acting and_____ as he did.

（A）speaking

（B）speak

（C）his speaking

（D）to speak

＜解答＞ A（連接詞平行構句）

85. Since their organization has not followed the budgetary reforms we did, their gross revenues were less this year_____.

（A）than us

（B）as ours

（C）than ours

（D）but also ours

＜解答＞ C（比較）

86. The fruit delivered directly from the orchard was_____ also delicious.

（A）not only ripe and

（B）not only ripe but

（C）only ripe

（D）as ripe as but

＜解答＞ B（連接詞平行構句）

87. When I stop to consider my ambitions, I realize my main goals consist of doing well in school, graduating, and_____.

（A）to make money

（B）making money

（C）be making money

（D）make money

＜解答＞ B（平行構句）

88. The risk the financial commission is taking is_____.

    (A) greater than the bank

    (B) as greater than the bank's

    (C) greater than the bank's

    (D) as greater as the bank's

    <解答> C（比較）

89. The main sports at the college were_____, and baseball.

    (A) archery, to ride

    (B) archery, ride

    (C) to archery, ride

    (D) archery, riding

    <解答> D（平行構句）

90. The diplomat found the situation of being caught on the border during the fighting_____ exhilarating.

    (A) both terrifying but also

    (B) both terrifying and

    (C) as terrifying as also

    (D) not only terrifying and

    <解答> B（連接詞形式）

91. The chemist placed the bowl_____ the two test tubes.

    (A) among

    (B) between

    (C) in

    (D) through

    <解答> B（介詞）

92. _____ the symphony, no one in the audience spoke.

    (A) By

    (B) For

    (C) During

    (D) From

　＜解答＞　C（介詞）

93.　The rain fell so heavily that it leaked＿＿＿ the ceiling.

（A）at

（B）over

（C）since

（D）through

　＜解答＞　D（介詞）

94.　In the Eastern Hemisphere, the eclipse of the sun occurred＿＿＿ mid-June.

（A）on

（B）in

（C）from

（D）until

　＜解答＞　B（介詞）

95.　The irate citizen kept a record of all the unauthorized buses that came＿＿＿ the residestial street.

（A）at

（B）for

（C）above

（D）down

　＜解答＞　D（介詞）

96.　The more students understand the concepts of gemetry, the easier it is for ＿＿＿ to appreciate the scientific achievements built on these formulas.

（A）one

（B）them

（C）him

（D）her

　＜解答＞　B（代名詞一致性）

97.　When the contest was over and the results were posted, the team members were so exhausted they couldn't even read＿＿＿.

（A）it

(B) them

(C) themselves

(D) us

<解答> B（代名詞一致性）

98.　The child to_____ she was kind, grew up to be one of our most distinguished

teachers in this area.

(A) whom

(B) which

(C) us

(D) them

<解答> A（代名詞一致性）

99.　Have you ever caught us giving_____ an underserved congratulations for

doing well on a project？

(A) yourself

(B) themselves

(C) ourselves

(D) itself

<解答> C（代名詞一致性）

100.　The clients have only_____ to blame if the paper does not include the

advertisement, because they submitted it too late for the advertising agency to

use.

(A) themselves

(B) ourselves

(C) itself

(D) yourself

<解答> A（代名詞一致性）

101.　We hoped_____ being there would give our cause credibility.

(A) he

(B) his

(C) him

（D）himself

＜解答＞ B（代名詞形式）

102. _____ arrival made it easier for us.

（A）Him

（B）He

（C）Himself

（D）His

＜解答＞ D（代名詞形式）

103. In her notebook, _____ has written herself a short note.

（A）her

（B）her one

（C）hers

（D）she

＜解答＞ D（代名詞形式）

104. We don't like to think of_____ in that way.

（A）us

（B）we

（C）ourselves

（D）our

＜解答＞ C（代名詞形式）

105. _____ ears could not believe what I was hearing.

（A）Mine

（B）My

（C）Myself

（D）Me

＜解答＞ B（代名詞形式）

106. The realtor sent the homeowner several inquiries_____ his property.

（A）asking about

（B）questioning him on

（C）concerning

（D）with questions on

＜解答＞ C（避免冗長）

107. Cups, plates, and＿＿＿ were replaced on the shelf.

（A）saucers

（B）tableware

（C）dishes

（D）pottery

＜解答＞ A（主詞平行構句）

108. Even though I was afraid before I began speaking, my voice was hearty and＿＿＿.

（A）vigorous

（B）dynamic

（C）energetic

（D）clear

＜解答＞ D（形容詞）

109. The editorial staff＿＿＿ and finished the first draft.

（A）terminated

（B）ended

（C）completed

（D）corrected

＜解答＞ D（動詞）

110. The investigator extracted the necessary information from the witness by＿＿＿ it.

（A）withdrawing

（B）asking for

（C）pulling

（D）removing

＜解答＞ B（修飾片語）

111. ＿＿＿ question was not relevant to the research.

（A）That it

（B）That

（C）Which it is

（D）That is the

＜解答＞ B（主詞）

112. The struggle of entrepreneurs＿＿＿ to be financially independent.

（A）which is

（B）are

（C）is

（D）are being

＜解答＞ C（動詞一致性）

113. When the crowd returned to their seats, ＿＿＿＿ started his speech again.

（A）this is the speaker

（B）the speaker who

（C）the speaker

（D）the speakers

＜解答＞ C（主詞）

114. As＿＿＿＿ leave, the security guard counts the number of visitors to the monument.

（A）the groups

（B）them

（C）the group

（D）their

＜解答＞ A（主詞）

115. The New York Times＿＿＿＿ a prestigious paper.

（A）it is considered

（B）is considered

（C）which is

（D）which is considered

＜解答＞ B（動詞）

116. The woman being charged with tax evasion has insisted that her lawyer and accountant_____ present.

（A）have been

（B）be

（C）were

（D）are

＜解答＞ B（假設語氣）

117. The final recommendation was that the employee on probation_____ a special night class for one semester.

（A）has attended

（B）attended

（C）attends

（D）attend

＜解答＞ D（假設語氣）

118. The building contractors have asked that the unfinished project_____.

（A）is extended

（B）will be extended

（C）has been extended

（D）be extended

＜解答＞ D（假設語氣）

119. The politician urged that all citizens_____ to the polls on election day.

（A）goes

（B）went

（C）must go

（D）go

＜解答＞ D（假設語氣）

120. The fire department ordered that the elevator_____.

（A）be turned off

（B）turn off

（C）was turned off

（D）turned off

<解答> A（假設語氣）

121.	_____ was not the way the event happened.

（A）What the press reported

（B）What reporteDthe press

（C）What reported

（D）The press reported

<解答> A（名詞附屬子句）

122.	It is a fact_____.

（A）that we all have to eat

（B）that all we have to eat

（C）that we all have ate

（D）all we have to eat

<解答> A（名詞附屬子句）

123.	_____ is his own decision.

（A）When leaving

（B）When does he leave

（C）When he leaves

（D）He leaves

<解答> C（名詞附屬子句）

124.	That he gave a false name shows_____.

（A）that he was doing something

（B）he was doing something

（C）something he was doing

（D）doing something he was

<解答> A（主格子句）

125.	The family_____ are French.

（A）which live opposite our house

（B）who live opposite our house

（C）of living opposite our house

　　　　（D）live oppsite our house

　　　　＜解答＞　B（關係子句）

126.　Buildings_____ of brick last longer than those made of mud.

　　　　（A）which

　　　　（B）which they are made

　　　　（C）which are made

　　　　（D）are made

　　　　＜解答＞　C（形容詞附屬子句）

127.　The mouse_____ comes out at night to nibble at the cheese we leave as bait.

　　　　（A）whom lives in the wall

　　　　（B）whom the wall lives in

　　　　（C）that lives in the wall

　　　　（D）that live in the wall

　　　　＜解答＞　C（形容詞附屬子句）

128.　The corporation_____ first will host the delegation for lunch.

　　　　（A）whose plant we visit

　　　　（B）whose visit

　　　　（C）whose visit we plant

　　　　（D）whose we plant

　　　　＜解答＞　A（形容詞附屬子句）

129.　Malcolm wanted to take the exam_____.

　　　　（A）we fail

　　　　（B）us failed

　　　　（C）that failed

　　　　（D）that we failed

　　　　＜解答＞　D（形容詞附屬子句）

130.　Trade relations among the states, _____ improving, are currently at an ebb.

　　　　（A）constantly are

　　　　（B）which are constant

　　　　（C）which constantly

（D）which are constantly

<解答> D（形容詞附屬子句）

131. While tomatoes are in season, _____.

（A）and inexpensive

（B）they are inexpensive

（C）inexpensive

（D）besides inexpensive

<解答> B（主要子句）

132. The governess agreed to teach the temperamental child_____ she was given complete authority.

（A）whether

（B）for

（C）that

（D）provided

<.解答.> D（連接詞形式+副詞子句）

133. _____, the graduate student who was late every day will still take the test.

（A）You think it wise

（B）You think it wise that

（C）Whether or not you think it wise

（D）Whether it wise

<解答> C（副詞附屬子句）

134. _____, the chorus should have learned the music by heart.

（A）By the time they rehearse

（B）By the time rehearse

（C）By the time they will rehearse

（D）They rehearse by the time

<解答> A（副詞附屬子句）

135. _____ there will be a change in administrations.

（A）In she wins

（B）She wins

（C）In the event she wins

（D）She wins the event

＜解答＞ C（副詞附屬子句）

136. The phone_____ started ringing.

（A）which next door

（B）was next door

（C）next door

（D）it was next door

＜解答＞ D（縮減的形容詞子句）

137. The sympathetic audience understood the man's speech, no matter how_____.

（A）it slurs

（B）slurred

（C）it was slur

（D）slurs

＜解答＞ B（縮減的形容詞子句）

138. The letter_____ our guests' intention to visit came after their arrival.

（A）it announcing

（B）announcing

（C）haDannounced

（D）having announced

＜解答＞ B（縮減的形容詞子句）

139. My best friend, _____ quickly, told the teacher I was home sick.

（A）who thinking

（B）be thinking

（C）think

（D）thinking

＜解答＞ D（縮減的形容詞子句）

140. The man_____ the wheelbarrow ignored our calls.

（A）who pushing

（B）pushing

（C）was pushing

（D）be who pushed

＜解答＞ B（縮減的形容詞子句）

141. _____, flowers need a lot of sun and water.

（A）When growth

（B）When they growing

（C）They are growing

（D）When growing

＜解答＞ D（縮減的副詞子句）

142. The sailer, home at last, is happy_____.

（A）he be sitting in the garden

（B）whenever sitting in the garden

（C）in the garden sitting

（D）whenever sit in the garden

＜解答＞ B（縮減的副詞子句）

143. _____, the commissioners like to take a walk.

（A）After they eating

（B）Eating

（C）After eating

（D）After to be eaten

＜解答＞ A（縮減的副詞子句）

144. _____, the mind lets suppressed thoughts surface.

（A）While we dream

（B）While dreaming

（C）While we dreaming

（D）While the mind it dreams

＜解答＞ A（縮減的副詞子句）

145. The fireman ran into the burning building_____ would not collapse.

（A）to be hoping

（B）hoping

（C）him hoping

（D）hoping it

＜解答＞ D（縮減的副詞子句）

146. Most universities_____ only people entering the freshman class.

（A）will be accepted

（B）accept

（C）although it accepts

（D）accepting

＜解答＞ B（動詞）

147. The debate_____ by the partisan review drew a large crowd.

（A）sponsored

（B）was sponsored

（C）has sponsored

（D）sponsoring

＜解答＞ A（動詞）

148. The permission that was needed to build the roads_____.

（A）it will be granted

（B）was granted

（C）was being granted

（D）have been granted

＜解答＞ B（動詞）

149. The song had a melody that_____ like this.

（A）was gone

（B）went

（C）is to go

（D）had went

＜解答＞ B（動詞）

150. The reasons_____ the proposal were numerous.

（A）although to reject

（B）for to reject

（C）for rejected

（D）for rejecting

　＜解答＞　D（修飾片語）

151.　The naive man_____ believed what he read in the papers.

（A）foolish

（B）foolishly

（C）fool

（D）fooled

　＜解答＞　B（易混淆的字家族）

152.　The gardens which were planted this spring should_____ the roadway.

（A）beautifully

（B）beautiful

（C）beauty

（D）beautify

　＜解答＞　D（易混淆的字家族）

153.　The major_____ were reported by the press without bias.

（A）eventual

（B）eventually

（C）eventful

（D）events

　＜解答＞　D（易混淆的字家族）

154.　The bodybuilder_____ tossed the child into the air.

（A）easily

（B）easy

（C）ease

（D）eased

　＜解答＞　A（易混淆的字家族）

155.　The first in_____ was the general who served his country only during peacetime.

（A）commander

（B）commandment

（C）commanding

（D）command

　　＜解答＞　D（易混淆的字家族）

156.　Never_____ such a night.

（A）I did see

（B）have I seen

（C）have seen I

（D）I saw

　　＜解答＞　B（主詞和動詞的位置）

157.　It_____ that the days seem to be getting shorter.

（A）not my imagination

（B）is not my imagination

（C）not is my imagination

（D）that is not my imagination

　　＜解答＞　B（主詞和動詞的位置）

158.　Among the rafters overhead_____.

（A）hung the bats

（B）the bate hanging

（C）bats was hung

（D）hang bats

　　＜解答＞　A（主詞和動詞的位置）

159.　He was told under no circumstances_____ the computer.

（A）he may use

（B）he use may

（C）may he use

（D）may use

　　＜解答＞　C（主詞和動詞的位置）

160.　Only once before_____.

（A）has happened this

（B）happened this

（C）this has happened

（D）has this happened

＜解答＞　A（主詞和動詞的位置）

161.　_____ are often used for laboratory experiments.

（A）Gray small mice

（B）That gray small mice

（C）They are small gray mice

（D）Small gray mice

＜解答＞　D（形容詞的位置）

162.　The young artist creates_____.

（A）translucent marble sculptures

（B）marble translucent sculptures

（C）marble sculptures translucent

（D）translucent sculptures marble

＜解答＞　A（形容詞的位置）

163.　My father, the_____ person, managed to fix the toaster.

（A）world's least mechanical

（B）least mechanical in the world

（C）least world's mechanical

（D）least mechanical world's

＜解答＞　A（形容詞的位置）

164.　The woman who lost the key hoped the finder would turn it over to_____.

（A）anyone official

（B）official anyone

（C）official

（D）anyone officially

＜解答＞　A（形容詞的位置）

165.　The trash can behind the juice stand was full of_____.

（A）ripe banana skins

（B）banana ripe skins

（C）ripe skins banana

（D）skins banana ripe

＜解答＞ A（形容詞的位置）

166. The secretary opened the mail which_____ that morning.

（A）had delivered

（B）delivered

（C）had been delivered

（D）is delivered

＜解答＞ C（被動語態）

167. In spite of popular support, the radio program_____ off the air very soon.

（A）had been taken

（B）will be taken

（C）takes

（D）were taken

＜解答＞ B（被動語態）

168. Strange things_____ by seemingly resonable people under stress.

（A）have done

（B）does

（C）is done

（D）are done

＜解答＞ D（被動語態）

169. Some people believe that giving gifts is one way_____ by others.

（A）to love

（B）love

（C）to be loved

（D）is loved

＜解答＞ C（被動語態）

170. Government control of the press_____ by every concerned citizens.

（A）has been opposed

（B）has opposed

（C）has been opposing

（D）opposed

＜解答＞ A（被動語態）

171. _____ Nantucket Island is a superb spot for watching the eclipse.

（A）A

（B）An

（C）The

（D）0

＜解答＞ D（冠詞）

172. We loved_____ Lake Geneva especially in the fall.

（A）a

（B）an

（C）the

（D）0

＜解答＞ D（冠詞）

173. Mrs. James did not arrive until sometime in_____ late afternoon.

（A）a

（B）an

（C）the

（D）0

＜解答＞ C（冠詞）

174. Western art of the 19th century shows the influence of_____ Far East.

（A）a

（B）an

（C）the

（D）0

＜解答＞ C（冠詞）

175. ＿＿＿ Air and Space Museum has the highest attendance record of all the museums in the world.

（A）A

（B）An

（C）The

（D）0

＜解答＞ C（冠詞）

176. One of the＿＿＿ inventions of the century was the holograph.

（A）cleverest than

（B）cleverer

（C）more clever

（D）most clever

＜解答＞ D（比較）

177. Langurage policy has been a subject of＿＿＿ debate in multilingual nations.

（A）sharp

（B）sharper

（C）sharpest

（D）more sharp

＜解答＞ A（比較）

178. The plan calls for a＿＿＿ defence than the one we currently have.

（A）stronger

（B）most strongest

（C）stronger than

（D）as stronger

＜解答＞ A（比較）

179. The water temperature surrounding the kelp beds is＿＿＿ than that around reefs.

（A）cool

（B）coolest

（C）more cool

(D) cooler

＜解答＞ D（比較）

180. When allowed to sleep, volunteers who were kept awake as many as 100 hours dreamed_____ than usual.

(A) more considerably

(B) considerably

(C) most

(D) most considerably

＜解答＞ B（比較）

181. If Marie_____, tell her I will call her back as soon as I return.

(A) calls

(B) called

(C) will call

(D) is going to call

＜解答＞ A（條件句）

182. The boy's parents knew he_____ if he had passed the final exam.

(A) graduated

(B) would graduate

(C) could have graduated

(D) will graduate

＜解答＞ C（條件句）

183. If_____ enough interest, the proposed flexible work schedule will be implemented.

(A) there be

(B) there will be

(C) there are

(D) there is

＜解答＞ D（條件句）

184. If it_____ rain, the band's members will have to cover their instruments.

(A) will start

（B）starts to

（C）started

（D）had started

＜解答＞　B（條件句）

185.　If the art dealer＿＿＿ the money, he would have bought the painting.

（A）had had

（B）has

（C）had

（D）would have

＜解答＞　A（條件句）

186.　Relief organizations have contributed＿＿＿ money to famine in Africa.

（A）both time and

（B）neither and

（C）time but

（D）time nor

＜解答＞　A（連接詞形式）

187.　The politician acted＿＿＿ about minority rights.

（A）as if she cared

（B）and if she cared

（C）if she cared

（D）either she cared

＜解答＞　A（連接詞形式）

188.　The Olympic judges thought the contestant ran the race＿＿＿.

（A）easily and well

（B）easy but good

（C）easily nor well

（D）easily and good

＜解答＞　A（連接詞形式）

189.　Not only the workers＿＿＿ the management are going to the union meeting.

（A）or

（B）also

（C）but also

（D）and

＜解答＞　C（連接詞形式）

190.　This particular comet, which comes every 10 years, does not move ＿＿＿＿ light.

（A）as quicker than

（B）as quickly as

（C）but quickly than

（D）as quickly

＜解答＞　B（連接詞形式）

191.　In the future, the discovery which will most change the lives of people, most affect the health of the world, and＿＿＿＿ the drug industry is the cure for the common cold.

（A）most change

（B）most changing

（C）with most change on

（D）most change of

＜解答＞　A（平行構句）

192.　The physician considers going to bed early to be more sensible＿＿＿＿.

（A）but staying up late

（B）than to stay up late

（C）than staying up lately

（D）than staying up late

＜解答＞　D（平行構句）

193.　Although we have reason to believe otherwise, the editors believe they can write＿＿＿＿.

（A）as well as we do

（B）as well we do

（C）well as we do

（D）as well than we do

＜解答＞ A（平行構句）

194. _____ nor the faculty appreciated her negative remarks.

（A）The administration

（B）Both the administration

（C）Neither the administration

（D）Either the administration

＜解答＞ C（平行構句）

195. The Empire State Building is quite tall, _____ the World Trade Center.

（A）and so is

（B）and as is

（C）as

（D）than so is

＜解答＞ A（平行構句）

196. The doctor sat_____ to the exit in case he had to leave early.

（A）next

（B）through

（C）out

（D）to

＜解答＞ A（介詞）

197. The bird flew_____ the treetops.

（A）opposite

（B）with

（C）up

（D）over

＜解答＞ D（介詞）

198. The moment the curtain fell, the audience rushed_____ the steps.

（A）on

（B）through

（C）up

（D）out

＜解答＞ C（介詞）

199. The politician's constituency was very upset_____ his announcement.

（A）out of

（B）from

（C）by

（D）behind

＜解答＞ C（介詞）

200. The parking lot_____ the restaurant was full.

（A）across from

（B）out of

（C）between

（D）from

＜解答＞ A（介詞）

201. Working with computers is the best way to learn_____ capabilities.

（A）our

（B）its

（C）their

（D）his

＜解答＞ C（代名詞一致性）

202. The way he talked, you would have thought the prize was his, although it was obviously_____, since I won it in front of them all.

（A）yours

（B）theirs

（C）ours

（D）mine

＜解答＞ D（代名詞一致性）

203. If you ask me for_____ next week, I will have time to find one.

（A）it

（B）our

（C）whom

（D）you

<解答> A（代名詞一致性）

204. The Secretary's peers did not approve of his decision to leave Congress since_____ feared a replacement would be hard to find.

（A）they

（B）it

（C）we

（D）you

<解答> A（代名詞一致性）

205. The jaws of the shark were so huge that we estimated a small craft could be damaged if_____ had the misfortune to encounter the beast in the ocean.

（A）he

（B）it

（C）you

（D）they

<解答> B（代名詞一致性）

206. The senator collects facts for his memories by writing notes to_____.

（A）his own

（B）his

（C）himself

（D）he

<解答> C（代名詞形式）

207. One of_____ has to take responsibility for the act.

（A）our

（B）us

（C）we

（D）ourselves

<解答> B（代名詞形式）

208. They taught_____ to read Latin from the old grammar book.

（A）themselves

（B）they

（C）their

（D）there

＜解答＞　A（代名詞形式）

209.　Knowing one's score on the first test, ＿＿＿＿ is apt to do better the second time.

（A）one

（B）it

（C）she

（D）he

＜解答＞　A（代名詞形式）

210.　Giving credit where＿＿＿＿ was deserved, the principal handed over the award.

（A）it

（B）itself

（C）it's

（D）its

＜解答＞　A（代名詞形式）

211.　The student's stipend gave him more than enough＿＿＿＿ his needs.

（A）for

（B）oversupplying

（C）in excess of

（D）that was too much for

＜解答＞　A（避免冗長）

212.　The hot day was remarkable for its＿＿＿＿.

（A）heat

（B）humidity

（C）scorching temperature

（D）warmth

<解答> B（避免冗長）

213.　The class started_____ the book.

　　（A）to begin

　　（B）at the beginning of

　　（C）commencing with

　　（D）to set about

　　<解答> B（避免冗長）

214.　The doorman admitted him by_____.

　　（A）letting him in

　　（B）unlocking the door

　　（C）allowing him to enter

　　（D）permitting his entry

　　<解答> B（避免冗長）

215.　Peter borrows from and_____ his friends.

　　（A）then repays

　　（B）uses the credit of

　　（C）takes loans from

　　（D）is in debt to

　　<解答> A（避免冗長）

216.　The foot and the ankle are the parts of the body system_____.

　　（A）that aid in walking

　　（B）aid in walking

　　（C）that walking

　　（D）walking

　　<解答> A（主詞）

217.　_____, the windy city, is the home for the skyscraper.

　　（A）Chicago which is

　　（B）Chicago it

　　（C）This is Chicago

　　（D）Chicago

<解答> D（主詞）

218. _____, which is a difficult task, requires balance.

（A）Crossing the footbridge

（B）The footbridge

（C）Across the footbridge

（D）The footbridge that is

<解答> A（主詞）

219. When all the trainees reasembled, the foreman_____ showed them how to work the new drill.

（A）who had been practicing

（B）who practicing

（C）he who had practicing

（D）what had practiced

<解答> A（主詞）

220. The_____ decided to return to their hotel for a rest after a day of sightseeing.

（A）tourists were

（B）tourist

（C）tourists had been

（D）tourists

<解答> D（主詞）

221. Before a member can make a motion, it is necessary that he_____ the presiding officer.

（A）rise and address

（B）will rise and address

（C）rises and addresses

（D）rise and addresses

<解答> A（假設語氣）

222. The committee voted that all its members_____ a raise next year.

（A）will be given

（B）are going to be given

（C）be given

（D）have been given

<解答> C（假設語氣）

223. It is important that someone searching for a job＿＿＿ all the prospects.

（A）consider

（B）be considering

（C）considers

（D）will be considering

<解答> A（假設語氣）

224. The U. S. Immigration Service requires that all passengers＿＿＿ a passport.

（A）will have

（B）have

（C）must have

（D）shoulDhave

<解答> B（假設語氣）

225. The ad hoc committee proposed that the chairman＿＿＿.

（A）promote

（B）was promoted

（C）be promoted

（D）be promoting

<解答> C（假設語氣）

226. No announcement has been made concerning＿＿＿ on the next shuttle flight.

（A）who go

（B）who is going

（C）is who going

（D）who gone

<解答> B（名詞附屬子句）

227. Regarding our current Director of Finance, ＿＿＿ is of no consequence to me.

（A）he goes or stays

（B）whether he goes or stays

（C）whether he go or stays

（D）he goes whether he stays

＜解答＞ B（名詞附屬子句）

228. The prosecutor questioned the witness about_____.

（A）what knew he

（B）what did he knew

（C）he knew

（D）what he knew

＜解答＞ D（名詞附屬子句）

229. _____ the election is the question both political parties are asking.

（A）Who's candidate will win

（B）Whose candidate will win

（C）Whose will win the candidate

（D）Candidate will win

＜解答＞ B（名詞附屬子句）

230. The reasons given for postponing the meeting until next week suggested _____ unprepared.

（A）the managers

（B）to the managers

（C）how the managers were

（D）that the managers were

＜解答＞ D（名詞附屬子句）

231. The team_____ waiting for finally arrived.

（A）who been

（B）whom we had

（C）who we

（D）we had been

＜解答＞ D（形容詞附屬子句）

232. Statistics_____ substantiated by research are considered vailed.

（A）are

（B）which

（C）which are

（D）that be

＜解答＞ B（形容詞附屬子句）

233. The president refused to accept the decision_____.

（A）which the committee proposed

（B）proposed the committee

（C）which proposed the committee

（D）who the committee proposed

＜解答＞ A（形容詞附屬子句）

234. The author eagerly anticipates the time_____ finished, and she can start a new one.

（A）when her book

（B）when her book is

（C）her book be

（D）her will be

＜解答＞ B（形容詞附屬子句）

235. The economic recession was the focus of the debate, _____.

（A）surprises to no one

（B）no one was surprised

（C）which surprised no one

（D）to no one was surprised

＜解答＞ C（形容詞附屬子句）

236. The applicant was turned down by the college_____ were too low.

（A）his test scores

（B）because

（C）because his test scores

（D）if test scores

＜解答＞ C（副詞附屬子句）

237.	＿＿ the rain has stopped, the field will dry out.

（A）Though

（B）While

（C）Even if

（D）Now that

＜解答＞ D（副詞附屬子句）

238.	The service attendant filled the tires＿＿ could ride our bikes.

（A）as we

（B）so that we

（C）even if we

（D）so that

＜解答＞ B（副詞附屬子句）

239.	The meeting was postponed＿＿.

（A）although no reason was given

（B）no reason given

（C）why no reason was given

（D）although given no reason

＜解答＞ A（副詞附屬子句）

240.	＿＿ my brother, I don't have to believe everything he says.

（A）Even though he is

（B）So he is

（C）As

（D）Where he is

＜解答＞ A（副詞附屬子句）

241.	The chessmen, ＿＿, are displayed in a glass case.

（A）which from ivory

（B）which carved from ivory

（C）carved from ivory

（D）carving from ivory

＜解答＞ C（縮減的形容詞子句）

242. The noise of the trains_____ into the station was deafening.

（A）that come

（B）which was coming

（C）coming

（D）that coming

＜解答＞ C（縮減的形容詞子句）

243. A political campaign____ will be costly.

（A）which for months that

（B）lasts for months

（C）lasting for months

（D）will last for months

＜解答＞ C（縮減的形容詞子句）

244. The barn, _____ went up in flames.

（A）loaded with hay

（B）it was loading hay

（C）it loaded hay

（D）which loadeDwith hay

＜解答＞ A（縮減的形容詞子句）

245. The stock_____ in value should be sold.

（A）which has not increased

（B）has not increased

（C）not been increasing

（D）who has not increased

＜解答＞ A（形容詞附屬子句）

246. Pedestrians should look to the left and right_____ the street.

（A）when crossing

（B）when they be crossing

（C）they cross

（D）when to cross

＜解答＞ A（縮減的副詞子句）

247. _____, the nurse checked the patient's temperature.

（A）Called the doctor

（B）Before calling the doctor

（C）The doctor calling

（D）Before the doctor calling

＜解答＞ B（縮減的副詞子句）

248. _____, Michael always comes off worst in an agreement.

（A）Whether is right or wrong

（B）Whether right and wrong

（C）Whether right or wrong

（D）Whether is right and wrong

＜解答＞ C（副詞子句）

249. _____, the candidate checked his facts.

（A）Before making the speech

（B）Before he is making the speech

（C）Before the speech is making

（D）Making their speech

＜解答＞ A（縮減的副詞子句）

250. The deadline, _____, had been extended to accommodate our schedule.

（A）passing

（B）although past

（C）while being passed

（D）passed

＜解答＞ B（縮減的副詞子句）

251. _____, the examinees knew it was time to stop.

（A）Hearing the bell

（B）Heard the bell

（C）To have been heard the bell

（D）To hear the bell

＜解答＞ A（縮減的副詞子句）

252. Although the subscription department claims_____ our order, we are still getting the magazine.

(A) having received

(B) not receiving

(C) not to have received

(D) to have not received

<解答>　C（否定的不定詞）

253. The pilots____ the most direct route to save fuel.

(A) although choosing

(B) when they chose

(C) was to choose

(D) chose

<解答>　D（動詞）

254. One's success cannot always_____ in terms of money.

(A) be measured

(B) being measured

(C) to measured

(D) measure

<解答>　A（被動語態）

255. If the superintendent does not_____ his mind, there is nothing more to be done.

(A) changes

(B) have changed

(C) change

(D) to change

<解答>　C（動詞）

256. After_____ attempts, the police were able to enter the building.

(A) repeating

(B) repetition

(C) repeatedly

（D）repeated

＜解答＞ D（易混淆的字家族）

257. The values of a society are reflected in its_____.

　　（A）traditional

　　（B）traditions

　　（C）traditionally

　　（D）traditionalize

　　＜解答＞ B（易混淆的字家族）

258. Although the couch looks_____, it is extremely hard.

　　（A）comfortable

　　（B）comfortably

　　（C）comfortableness

　　（D）comfort

　　＜解答＞ A（易混淆的字家族）

259. The_____ of landing men on the moon is unsurpassed in modern technology.

　　（A）achieve

　　（B）achiever

　　（C）achievement

　　（D）achievable

　　＜解答＞ C（易混淆的字家族）

260. A family with 10 children in a small restaurant is easily_____.

　　（A）noticed

　　（B）notice

　　（C）notify

　　（D）notification

　　＜解答＞ A（易混淆的字家族）

261. There_____ the proofreader overlooked on this page.

　　（A）a mistake is

　　（B）is a mistake

　　（C）a mistake be

（D）be mistake

＜解答＞　B（主詞和動詞的位置）

262.　So little known_____ that the explorers had to proceed without maps.

（A）was the terrain

（B）the terrain was

（C）the terrain

（D）terrain was

＜解答＞　A（主詞和動詞的位置）

263.　Close by the door_____.

（A）the spy listen.

（B）listening the spy

（C）listened the spy

（D）the listening spy

＜解答＞　C（主詞和動詞的位置）

264.　Only when it rains_____.

（A）does the river overflow

（B）the river does overflow

（C）overflows does the river

（D）overflow the river

＜解答＞　A（主詞和動詞的位置）

265.　So little_____ that the neighbors could not settle their differences.

（A）they agreed

（B）agreed did they

（C）did they agree

（D）they did agree

＜解答＞　C（主詞和動詞的位置）

266.　The cost of_____ of both scientific and commercial interest may be prohibitive.

（A）large-scale projects research

（B）research large-scale

（C）projects research large-scale

（D）large-scale research projects

＜解答＞ D（形容詞＋副詞的位置）

267. The biological factor in food design requires_____.

（A）safe food and nutritious

（B）safe and nutritious food

（C）food safe and nutritious

（D）safe an food nutritious

＜解答＞ B（形容詞位置）

268. _____ would have known the answer.

（A）Anyone is clever

（B）Clever anyone

（C）Anyone clever

（D）Clever is anyone

＜解答＞ C（形容詞位置）

269. Nuclear power_____ is a risk to civilization.

（A）as a system total

（B）as a total system

（C）total system

（D）system total

＜解答＞ B（形容詞位置）

270. The shore is the home of the new rich and is dotted with_____.

（A）big great houses

（B）great big houses

（C）houses big great

（D）houses great big

＜解答＞ B（形容詞位置）

271. " You'll finish the work and go to see her, _____ ? "

（A）would you

（B）will you

（C）don't you

（D）are you

<解答> B（附加問語）

272. " What did you hear ? "

" We heard＿＿＿ long lecture that we were falling asleep. "

（A）such a

（B）too

（C）so

（D）such

<解答> A（形容詞）

273. " Where do you wish to go ? "

" I wish to go to the＿＿＿. "

（A）shoes stores

（B）shoes' store

（C）shoe store

（D）shoe's store

<解答> C（形容詞相等物亦即名詞當形容詞用）

274. " When will they leave ? "

" They＿＿＿ very soon. "

（A）do leave

（B）are leaving

（C）have left

（D）leave

<解答> B（動詞時態）

275. " What have you finished ? "

" I have finished＿＿＿. "

（A）a day work

（B）a day's work

（C）day's working

（D）a-day work

＜解答＞ B（所有形容詞）

276. " John, how are you today ? "

" I am＿＿＿ that I can meet you. "

（A）too glad

（B）very glad

（C）so glad

（D）such glad

＜解答＞ B（形容詞和副詞位置）

277. " What is your nationality ? "

" I am＿＿＿. "

（A）American

（B）The American

（C）Americans

（D）America

＜解答＞ A（名詞）

278. " She has called me by telephone this morning and said she wanted to see me. "

" Do you know＿＿＿ ? "

（A）why she's asking for

（B）why she asks for

（C）what she's asking for

（D）what's she asking for

＜解答＞ C（名詞附屬子句）

279. " I hope that John will not play basketball tomorrow. "

" Yes, I＿＿＿. "

（A）hope it

（B）hope

（C）hope that

（D）hope so

＜解答＞ D（縮減的名詞子句）

280. " What did you hear ? "

" I heard_____ the thunder. "

（A）a bolt of

（B）a flash of

（C）one of

（D）a piece of

＜解答＞ A（數量名詞+物質名詞）

281. " Why does everybody like Mrs. Mercer ? "

" Because Mrs. Mercer always_____ good after-dinner jokes. "

（A）says

（B）speaks

（C）talks

（D）tells

＜解答＞ D（動詞）

282. " As a matter of fact, I don't like the lady. "

" If the lady_____ actually a bother, I'll take her home. "

（A）are

（B）was

（C）is

（D）tells

＜解答＞ C（動詞一致性）

283. " What should we do ? "

" We wouldn't be in danger if you_____ to me. "

（A）had listened

（B）shall listen

（C）will listen

（D）have listened

＜解答＞ A（條件句）

284. " When did you eat ? "

" As soon as he came, we_____ our dinner. "

（A）must have eaten

（B）ate

（C）were eating

（D）had eaten

＜解答＞ B（動詞時態）

285. " You have to wait for ten weeks. "

" Ten weeks＿＿＿ too long for me to wait. "

（A）are

（B）is

（C）will

（D）shall be

＜解答＞ B（動詞一致性）

286. " I didn't catch the train. "

" You＿＿＿ the train if you had hurried. "

（A）would catch

（B）could catch

（C）could have caught

（D）had caught

＜解答＞ C（條件句）

287. " How can I clean my coat ? "

" You ought to have your coat＿＿＿. "

（A）clean and press

（B）cleaned and pressed

（C）cleaning and pressing

（D）cleaning and dressed

＜解答＞ B（過去分詞）

288. " I never wrote that letter. "

" Why do you have to deny＿＿＿ that letter. "

（A）writing

（B）to write

（C）write

（D）written

＜解答＞ A（易混淆的字家族）

289. " I can write English. "

" I would like to ask you_____ to study English. "

（A）when did you begun

（B）when did you begin

（C）when you began

（D）began

＜解答＞ C（副詞附屬子句）

290. " May I take the sports section ? "

" Sure, here_____. "

（A）is it

（B）is

（C）it

（D）it is

＜解答＞ D（主詞和動詞位置）

291. " Why do we have to be there at nine ? "

" The teacher demands that everyone_____ in his seat at nine o'clock. "

（A）will be

（B）should be

（C）be

（D）shall be

＜解答＞ C（假設語氣）

292. " She is going fishing tomorrow. "

" So_____. "

（A）I do

（B）do I

（C）and I

（D）I am

　　　<解答> C（主詞和動詞位置）

293.　" How did you come here. "

　　　" I came here_____ a car. "

　　（A）by

　　（B）on

　　（C）in

　　（D）of

　　　<解答> A（介詞）

294.　" When did you return home ? "

　　　" I returned home after I_____ my old friends. "

　　（A）would see

　　（B）have seen

　　（C）saw

　　（D）see

　　　<解答> C（動詞時態）

295.　" Whose fault ? "

　　　" The accident clearly resulted_____ your carelessness. "

　　（A）in

　　（B）on

　　（C）from

　　（D）for

　　　<解答> C（介詞）

296.　" What have happened to the train ? "

　　　" The train_____ a regular schedule. "

　　（A）runs over

　　（B）runs on

　　（C）runs out of

　　（D）runs into

　　　<解答> B（動詞+介詞）

297.　" How long ? "

" John_____ for you since noon. "

（A）waits

（B）is going to wait

（C）has been waiting

（D）had waited

＜解答＞ C（動詞時態）

298.　" My uncle can't speak English. "

　　　"　_____. "

（A）Either can't my aunt

（B）My aunt can neither

（C）Neither can my aunt

（D）Either my aunt can

＜解答＞ C（縮減的副詞子句）

299.　" How many books does she have ? "

　　　" She possesses_____ books. "

（A）plenty of

（B）a great deal of

（C）very much

（D）a quantity of

＜解答＞ A（形容詞）

300.　" Why didn't you give John some money ? "

　　　" If John had come, I_____ him that money. "

（A）have to give

（B）would give

（C）would have given

（D）would be giving

＜解答＞ C（條件句）

301.　" When did you go to work ? "

　　　" As soon as they came, we_____ to work. "

（A）went

（B）were going

（C）haDgone

（D）go

＜解答＞ A（動詞時態）

302. " Where did you find them ? "

" I found these things_____ a farm. "

（A）at

（B）in

（C）upon

（D）on

＜解答＞ D（介詞）

303. " When will Richard be home ? "

" Richard_____ one-fourth of his ROTC service by this time next year. "

（A）will complete

（B）will have completed

（C）is completing

（D）completes

＜解答＞ B（動詞時態）

304. " Then about the ice. "

" The ice melted _____. "

（A）fastly

（B）very fastly

（C）quick

（D）fast

＜解答＞ D（副詞）

305. " Is the sugar sweet ? "

" Yes, the sugar tastes_____. "

（A）very sweetly

（B）sweetness

（C）sweetly

（D）sweet

＜解答＞ D（易混淆的字家族）

306. " Do you see all your friends here ? "

" Everyone except＿＿＿. "

（A）he

（B）it

（C）they

（D）them

＜解答＞ D（代名詞形式）

307. " What did Joe do ? "

" He＿＿＿ asleep all morning. "

（A）lain

（B）laid

（C）lay

（D）lying

＜解答＞ C（動詞時態）

308. " What is your opinion ? "

" It is necessary that an employee＿＿＿ his work on time. "

（A）finishes

（B）finishs

（C）can finish

（D）finish

＜解答＞ D（假設語氣）

309. " What do you want ? "

" Would you please＿＿＿ me go there ? "

（A）allow

（B）enable

（C）permit

（D）let

＜解答＞ D（祈使語氣）

310. " You ought to have seen Jean last night. "

" Yes, I_____. "

（A）ought to

（B）should

（C）must

（D）should have

<解答> D（假設語氣）

311. " What did you say? "

" Women treat_____ men in a rather unsportsman like manner, don't you think ? "

（A）we

（B）our

（C）us

（D）me

<解答> C（代名詞形式）

312. " Who was arrested ? "

" None of the men_____ arrested. "

（A）was

（B）has been

（C）would be

（D）were

<解答> D（被動語態）

313. " What do you have to do tomorrow ? "

" I'll have to_____ in a conference. "

（A）join

（B）taking part

（C）attend

（D）participate

<解答> D（不定詞片語）

314. " What did you gct ? "

" I got a＿＿＿ bill. "

（A）twenty dollars

（B）twenty-dollars

（C）twenties-dollar

（D）twenty-dollar

＜解答＞ D（以名詞當形容詞用）

315. " What did you see ? "

" I saw Jin＿＿＿ the door. "

（A）to open

（B）open

（C）had opened

（D）opened

＜解答＞ B（沒有 to 的不定詞）

316. " Glad to visit you again. "

" Would you like＿＿＿ hot coffee ? "

（A）some

（B）any more

（C）any

（D）drink

＜解答＞ A（形容詞）

317. " I don't think he should stay. "

" Then, I'll make him＿＿＿ his plans. "

（A）changing

（B）to change

（C）changes

（D）change

＜解答＞ D（沒有 to 的不定詞）

318. " Why do you want to go to South America ? "

" It's because South America is＿＿＿ nice place that I like to visit there. "

（A）such a

（B）such

（C）so

（D）a very

<解答> A（形容詞）

319. " Would you tell me the news ? "

" I_____ as soon as I get a plane. "

（A）would

（B）would like

（C）will

（D）will like

<解答> C（動詞的一致性）

320. " Where is the chair ? "

" It's_____ window. "

（A）close the

（B）close to the

（C）close at the

（D）in the

<解答> B（形容詞+介詞）

321. " What do you want me to do ? "

" The radio is too loud, please turn it_____. "

（A）down

（B）out

（C）up

（D）over

<解答> A（動詞片語）

322. " Many people could play baseball. "

" _____. "

（A）So could you

（B）So you could

（C）You could so

（D）So you can

<解答> A（主詞和動詞位置）

323. " May I help you ? "

" Yes, I'd like to buy some＿＿＿. "

（A）blue furniture

（B）blue's furnitures

（C）blue furnitures

（D）blue's furniture

<解答> A（形容詞+不可數名詞）

324. " What will you do tomorrow ? "

" We are going＿＿＿ tomorrow. "

（A）to hunt

（B）hunting

（C）hunted

（D）hunt

<解答> B （易混淆的字家族）

325. " What do I have to do ? "

" The beds have to be＿＿＿. "

（A）made

（B）set

（C）taken

（D）done

<解答> A（被動語態）

326. " Are you coming to my party ? "

" If Professor Jone's coming, ＿＿＿. "

（A）so am I

（B）so would I

（C）I do so

（D）so I'll go

<解答> A（主詞和動詞位置）

327. " What has she done ? "

     " Does she have to collect_____ information ? "

     （A）many

     （B）much

     （C）a lot

     （D）a number of

     ＜解答＞ B（形容詞+不可數名詞）

328. " I'd like to go swimming. "

     " So_____. "

     （A）I do

     （B）do I

     （C）would I

     （D）had I

     ＜解答＞ C（主詞和動詞位置）

329. " Why are you so thirsty ? "

     " I drank_____ water than you. "

     （A）fewer

     （B）little

     （C）less

     （D）least

     ＜解答＞ C（比較）

330. " We didn't study mathematics last night. "

     " But you_____. "

     （A）had studied

     （B）could

     （C）should

     （D）could have

     ＜解答＞ D（縮減的副詞子句）

331. " Anybody will help me! "

     " Would you mind quitting_____? "

（A）to shout

（B）shout

（C）shouting

（D）shouted

＜解答＞　C（動名詞）

332.　" Where did he stop ? "

　　　" He stopped＿＿＿ Park Avenue. "

（A）by

（B）at

（C）in

（D）on

＜解答＞　D（介詞）

333.　" She is sick. "

　　　" How long＿＿＿ sick. "

（A）she is been

（B）she has been

（C）she is to be

（D）has she been

＜解答＞　D（主詞和動詞位置）

334.　" Why ? "

　　　" I don't like＿＿＿ toast. "

（A）a

（B）some

（C）those

（D）any

＜解答＞　D（形容詞）

335.　" He has to leave tomorrow. "

　　　" When he＿＿＿ tomorrow, please let me know. "

（A）will leave

（B）leaves

（C）could leave

（D）would leave

＜解答＞ B（動詞）

336. " I don't like this food. "

" _____ to eat your breakfast in the morning ? "

（A）Would you like

（B）Will you like

（C）Won't you like

（D）Do you like

＜解答＞ A（主詞和動詞位置）

337. " Where does he live ? "

" He lives _____ 144 Wall Street. "

（A）at

（B）in

（C）on

（D）by

＜解答＞ A（介詞）

338. " What color suitcase do you have ? "

" My suitcase has the same color _____ yours. "

（A）with

（B）from

（C）like

（D）as

＜解答＞ D（介詞）

339. " Wake up ! how long have you slept ? "

" I have slept all day long, _____ again ? "

（A）should have I slept

（B）should I sleep

（C）I should sleep

（D）should I have slept

<解答> B（主詞和動詞位置）

340. " I don't have time. "

" You should finish＿＿＿ the letter by noon. "

（A）to answer

（B）answering

（C）by answering

（D）answer

<解答> B（動名詞）

341. " I did go there. "

" What would you have done if you＿＿＿ to work yesterday ? "

（A）didn't have

（B）hadn't had

（C）didn't

（D）didn't have had

<解答> B（條件句）

342. " Where are the Smiths going to live ? "

" The Smiths are considering＿＿＿ to Chicago. "

（A）moving

（B）to move

（C）move

（D）moved

<解答> A（動名詞）

343. " I saw many children. "

" How many children＿＿＿ over there ? "

（A）did they play

（B）played they

（C）they played

（D）played

<解答> D（動詞）

344. " What interests you ? "

" The subject_____ I am interested is English. "

（A）in that

（B）in which

（C）for which

（D）in what

＜解答＞ B（連接詞＋動詞片語）

345.　" I never saw him play baseball. "

" He_____ to like anything. "

（A）is never going

（B）go never

（C）never go

（D）will go

＜解答＞ A（動詞和副詞位置）

346.　" Who permits him ? "

" I permit him_____. "

（A）that go

（B）for going

（C）to go

（D）go

＜解答＞ C（不定詞）

347.　" When will you return the money to me ? "

" I'll return it to you when I_____ you next Sunday. "

（A）see

（B）would see

（C）am going

（D）will see

＜解答＞ A（動詞）

348.　" How about the show ? "

" The show is_____. "

（A）amused

（B）amusing

（C）amusement

（D）amuse

<解答> B（易混淆的字家族）

349. " Do you know these people ? "

" We've met those people, _____ ? "

（A）have we

（B）didn't we

（C）haven't we

（D）did we

<解答> C（附加問題）

350. " I am afraid not. "

" I certainly didn't intend to cause you so_____ inconvenience. "

（A）more

（B）many

（C）much

（D）very

<解答> C（形容詞）

351. " Where does happiness come from ? "

" Happiness lies_____ trying to do one's duty. "

（A）of

（B）for

（C）in

（D）on

<解答> C（介詞）

352. " What did you say ? "

" You can_____ me. "

（A）count with

（B）count in

（C）count out

（D）count on

＜解答＞ D（動詞片語）

353. " Can you understand ? "

" You can speak to me_____ on that subject. "

（A）with plain

（B）plain

（C）plaining

（D）plainly

＜解答＞ D（副詞）

354. " How long ? "

" It is about fifteen-hour trip_____ plane. "

（A）at

（B）in

（C）over

（D）by

＜解答＞ D（介詞）

355. " What do they have ? "

"They have wonderful things_____ at this restaurant. "

（A）to eat

（B）eat

（C）to be eaten

（D）for eating

＜解答＞ A（介詞）

356. " I don't understand that sentence. "

" Let's get Tom_____ that sentence again. "

（A）cxplain

（B）explained

（C）explaining

（D）to explain

＜解答＞ D（不定詞）

357. " What will happen ? "

" By next June we_____ a million refrigerators. "

（A）will have sold

（B）sell

（C）shall

（D）will sel

＜解答＞ A（動詞時態）

358. " Do you know Jimmy? "

" Does Jimmy enjoy_____ ? "

（A）to dance

（B）dance

（C）dancing

（D）danced

＜解答＞ C（動名詞）

359. " What do you think about John ? "

" He has no sense_____. "

（A）wherever

（B）however

（C）nevertheless

（D）whatsoever

＜解答＞ D（形容詞）

360. " What will happen to him ? "

" Because he needs to take part in the TOEFL, he_____ to study tomorrow. "

（A）has

（B）wants

（C）likes

（D）should

＜解答＞ A（動詞）

361. " What is the difference ? "

" This material is different from_____. "

（A）your

（B）that

（C）that book

（D）that material

　　＜解答＞　B（代名詞）

362.　" Do you want to wait ? "

　　" Two weeks_____ too long for me to wait. "

（A）is

（B）are

（C）were

（D）was

　　＜解答＞　A（動詞）

363.　" What's the matter ? "

　　" I wonder_____. "

（A）where is my umbrella

（B）where my umbrella is

（C）is where my umbrella

（D）my umbrella is where

　　＜解答＞　B（名詞附屬子句）

364.　" What did he ask? "

　　" He asked me if John had the capability_____. "

（A）to do that

（B）to doing taht

（C）of doing that

（D）do that

　　＜解答＞　C（修飾片語）

365.　" I can do everything. "

　　" Don't act as if you_____ the only pebble on the beach. "

（A）are

（B）were

（C）have been

（D）would be

＜解答＞ B（假設語氣）

366. " Would you come to New York ? "

" I_____ as soon as I get the ticket. "

（A）would

（B）would like

（C）will

（D）will like

＜解答＞ C（動詞一致性）

367. " What ? "

" We danced_____ the music of Jimmy Dorsey's band. "

（A）to

（B）with

（C）in

（D）on

＜解答＞ A（介詞）

368. " Do you want to go with me ? "

" Yes, I_____. "

（A）want

（B）would like to

（C）wnat it

（D）want to

＜解答＞ B（動詞）

369. " Where's Mary ? "

"_____."

（A）There she is

（B）There Mary is

（C）Is there Mary

（D）There is she

<解答> A（主詞和動詞位置）

370.　" I wish to leave. "

　　" Don't you have anything else_____? "

　　（A）to be done

　　（B）to do

　　（C）do

　　（D）doing

　　<解答> B（不定詞）

371.　" Jean was not secretary. "

　　" No, _____. "

　　（A）Neither I was

　　（B）I was not neither

　　（C）I wasn't either

　　（D）Either wasn't I

　　<解答> C（動詞和副詞的位置）

372.　" Have you ever been in Rome ? "

　　" No, but that's the city_____. "

　　（A）I want most like to visit.

　　（B）I'd most like to visit

　　（C）which I like to visit most

　　（D）what I'd like most to visit

　　<解答> B（形容詞附屬子句）

373.　" How do you think about the breakfast ? "

　　" The breakfast is inferior_____ that of yesterday. "

　　（A）than

　　（B）to

　　（C）under

　　（D）with

　　<解答> B（介詞）

374.　" Did you talk to him ? "

" I_____ to him about this matter before it was brought up at the meeting. "

（A）would talk

（B）had talked

（C）was talking

（D）talked

＜解答＞ B（動詞時態）

375.　" When did you come here ? "

" I_____ here since August 25. "

（A）have been

（B）was

（C）have

（D）had been

＜解答＞ A（動詞時態）

376.　" What ? "

" There are some applications on the desk, _____? "

（A）isn't it

（B）is it

（C）aren't there

（D）is that so

＜解答＞ C（附加問題）

377.　" Let's go to the dinner right away. "

" It's important, _____? "

（A）aren't you

（B）isn't it

（C）you haven't

（D）is it

＜解答＞ B（附加問題）

378.　" John won't come tomorrow. "

" Did he say he_____ next week ? "

（A）will come

（B）would come

（C）is coming

（D）had come

　　<解答> B（名詞附屬子句）

379.　" Did you see any foreigner present at the party ? "

　　" He was the only foreigner_____ I saw at the party. "

（A）whom

（B）that

（C）who

（D）which

　　<解答> B（形容詞附屬子句）

380.　As you treat me_____ will I treat you.

（A）as

（B）so

（C）like

（D）and

　　<解答> B（連接詞）

381.　" What is your opinion ? "

　　" You have to leave them before you get_____. "

（A）involves

（B）involve

（C）involving

（D）involved

　　<解答> D（過去分詞）

382.　" Did you hear what_____ ? "

　　" I didn't hear that. "

（A）his uncle was heard

（B）his uncle hears

（C）his uncle heard

（D）his uncle have heard

<解答>　C（名詞附屬子句）

383.　" It's a small steak cooked over a grill. "

　　　" What is this minute steak that's＿＿＿ the menu ? "

　　　（A）over

　　　（B）on

　　　（C）in

　　　（D）at

　　　<解答>　B（介詞）

384.　" Good morning, Bill. "

　　　" Did you have any trouble＿＿＿ through the snow ? "

　　　（A）drove

　　　（B）drive

　　　（C）driving

　　　（D）to drive

　　　<解答>　C（現在分詞）

385.　" A man was killed? "

　　　" Where is the body of the＿＿＿ man ? "

　　　（A）murder

　　　（B）murdered

　　　（C）murdering

　　　（D）having murder

　　　<解答>　B（過去分詞）

386.　" What did he have put on his itinerary ? "

　　　" He had Chicago＿＿＿ on his intinerary. "

　　　（A）put

　　　（B）to put

　　　（C）to be put

　　　（D）putting

　　　<解答>　A（動詞時態）

387.　" Where is she sitting ? "

" She is sitting_____ me. "

（A）near to

（B）next by

（C）next

（D）next to

＜解答＞ D（介詞）

388. " What about the complaints ? "

" She's taken all those books away, _____ she ? "

（A）isn't

（B）doesn't

（C）hasn't

（D）is

＜解答＞ C（附加問題）

389. " What do you want me to do ? "

" The walls need_____. "

（A）to paint

（B）to painting

（C）to be paint

（D）painting

＜解答＞ D（動名詞）

390. " It seems to be very crowed. "

" How many passengers are_____ the train. "

（A）in

（B）with

（C）at

（D）on

＜解答＞ D（介詞）

391. " Why did Professor Baker come here ? "

" She asked that he_____ to leave for Chicago. "

（A）had

（B）have

（C）has

（D）will have

<解答> B（假設語氣）

392. " Why didn't you meet Frank ? "

" If you had told me in advance, I_____ him. "

（A）would meet

（B）would had meet

（C）would have met

（D）would have meet

<解答> C（條件句）

393. " The United States in certainly an interesting country, isn't it ? "

" Yes, you can find just about_____ there. "

（A）something

（B）nothing

（C）everything

（D）anything

<解答> C（名詞）

394. " I did not see you last night. "

" I wish I_____ you last night. "

（A）met

（B）would meet

（C）could have met

（D）have met

<解答> C（假設語氣）

395. " What is the chairman's duty ? "

" The chairman should help all the members_____ the committee. "

（A）in

（B）on

（C）at

（D）inside

　　＜解答＞　B（介詞）

396.　" What do you expect now ? "

　　" I am looking forward to_____ the play. "

　　（A）see

　　（B）saw

　　（C）have seen

　　（D）seeing

　　＜解答＞　D（動詞片語＋動名詞）

397.　" What did your sister say ? "

　　" She_____ me a question. "

　　（A）asked

　　（B）explained

　　（C）helped

　　（D）said

　　＜解答＞　A（動詞）

398.　" What gate should I go through ? "

　　" You should go to_____. "

　　（A）gate three

　　（B）third gate

　　（C）three gate

　　（D）gate third

　　＜解答＞　A（名詞＋數量形容詞）

399.　" Are you going to see him ? "

　　" If the boy goes, _____. "

　　（A）I do so

　　（B）so will I

　　（C）so goes I

　　（D）so I'll go

　　＜解答＞　B（倒裝句）

400. " What do you have to do ? "

" I have a pair of slacks to_____ the cleaners. "

（A）he send to

（B）send to

（C）be sent to

（D）sending to

＜解答＞ B（不定詞）

401. " What do you think about French ? "

" If I had known French was so difficult, I_____ it up. "

（A）would never taken

（B）would never take

（C）will never take

（D）would never have taken

＜解答＞ B（條件句）

402. " Where are you going ? "

" I am going to the_____. "

（A）oranges' juice store

（B）oranges juice store

（C）orange's juice store

（D）orange juice store

＜解答＞ D（形容詞相等物亦即名詞當形容詞用）

403. " Do they like Mary ? "

" Sure, she is_____ girl. "

（A）a such nice

（B）so nice

（C）such a nice

（D）such nice

＜解答＞ C（形容詞）

404. " I was very tired. "

" You would be less tired if you_____ to be earlier. "

（Ａ）had gone

（Ｂ）go

（Ｃ）went

（Ｄ）have gone

　＜解答＞　Ｃ（條件句）

405.　" Did you have to go ? "

　　　" I_____ to go anyway. "

（Ａ）would

（Ｂ）could

（Ｃ）might

（Ｄ）had

　＜解答＞　Ｄ（動詞時態）

406.　" Money. "

　　　" Do you plan to let Mr. Johson_____ that money ? "

（Ａ）have

（Ｂ）to have

（Ｃ）having

（Ｄ）to possess

　＜解答＞　Ａ（沒有 to 的不定詞）

407.　" I do like all the holidays. "

　　　" What holidays_____ in your country ? "

（Ａ）are celebrated

（Ｂ）celebrating

（Ｃ）celebrated

（Ｄ）celebrate

　＜解答＞　Ａ（被動語態）

408.　" You ought to have seen your sister last night. "

　　　" Yes, I_____. "

（Ａ）ought to

（Ｂ）should

（C）must

（D）should have

＜解答＞　D（動詞）

409.　" How can I sleep ? "

　　　" In order to get a good night's sleep, put a Do Not＿＿＿ sign on the door. "

　　　（A）Disturb

　　　（B）Upset

　　　（C）Yell

　　　（D）Cry

　　　＜解答＞　A（祈使法語氣）

410.　" I'd like to cut you hair. "

　　　" If you＿＿＿ to cut my hair, how short would you make it ? "

　　　（A）were

　　　（B）could

　　　（C）are

　　　（D）would

　　　＜解答＞　A（假設語氣）

411.　" What do you want to drink ? "

　　　" Let's have the waiter＿＿＿ some milk. "

　　　（A）bring

　　　（B）to bring

　　　（C）bringing

　　　（D）brought

　　　＜解答＞　A（沒有 to 的不定詞）

412.　" How're we going ? "

　　　" Do you know how far＿＿＿ from New York to Chicago ? "

　　　（A）it will be

　　　（B）it is

　　　（C）won't it be

　　　（D）is it

<解答> B（名詞附屬子句）

413. " How have the boys spent their vacation ? "

" Most of them have spent their time_____ playing baseball. "

（A）by

（B）on

（C）in

（D）at

<解答> A（介詞）

414. " Do you mind closing the window ? "

" _____, for we have enough fresh air. "

（A）No, I don't mind

（B）Yes, I don't

（C）No, I do

（D）No, I don't

<解答> D（簡短回答）

415. " What happens to this machine ? "

" It needs to be_____. "

（A）heat

（B）heated

（C）hot

（D）hotted

<解答> B（被動語態）

416. " They must like that very pretty girl. "

" Yes, I imagine_____. "

（A）to

（B）that

（C）her

（D）so

<解答> D（縮減的副詞子句）

417. " I was late again this morning. "

" Well, I think you had better_____ on time. "

（A）to start to be

（B）start being

（C）started being

（D）to be

＜解答＞ B（假設語氣）

418.　" Did you leave very early last night, Mr. Smith ? "

" Yes, but I wish I_____ so early.

（A）didn't leave

（B）hadn't left

（C）haven't left

（D）couldn't leave

＜解答＞ B（假設語氣）

419.　" Who are they ? "

" Don't you know_____ all of them are efficient ? "

（A）language's teachers

（B）languages teachers

（C）teaching language

（D）language teachers

＜解答＞ D（名詞當形容詞用）

420.　" Have you found your book yet ? "

" I'm not sure_____ I could have done with it. "

（A）whether

（B）what

（C）why

（D）where

＜解答＞ B（名詞附屬子句）

421.　" What do you want to do ? "

" I think_____ it myself. "

（A）I'd better to drive

（B）better I drive

（C）I'd rather drive

（D）I had drive better

＜解答＞ C（名詞附屬子句）

422. " Did you go there ? "

" I_____ be there. "

（A）use of

（B）used to

（C）am used to

（D）was used to

＜解答＞ B（動詞時態）

423. " Ticket ? "

" Everyone who comes must_____ a ticket with him. "

（A）take

（B）bring

（C）get

（D）taking

＜解答＞ B（動詞）

424. " When do you wish to play baseball ? "

" We expected_____ at the churchyard. "

（A）playing

（B）played

（C）play

（D）to play

＜解答＞ D（不定詞）

425. " Is Jean always punctual ? "

" She is_____ slow she can't be in time for class all the time. "

（A）such

（B）too

（C）so

（D）yery

<解答> C（副詞）

426. " What do you want ? "

" I want_____ that is on the table. "

（A）the loaf of bread

（B）some bread

（C）a loaf of bread

（D）a bread

<解答> A（數量名詞+物質名詞）

427. " Why do you like that place ? "

" I_____ in that city. "

（A）borne

（B）bore

（C）hear

（D）was born

<解答> D（動詞）

428. " Are you going to mail him that watch ? "

" No, I must have it_____ first. "

（A）address

（B）addressing

（C）to be addressed

（D）addressed

<解答> D（過去分詞）

429. " I was there. "

"_____."

（A）So was Maggie

（B）Either was my parent

（C）Neither was Maggie

（D）Neither was my parent

<解答> A（主詞和動詞位置）

430. " Are you very happy now ? "

   " No, if I were I_____ work any longer. "

   （A）wouldn't

   （B）am not

   （C）won't

   （D）don't

   ＜解答＞ A（假設語氣）

431. " Do you have a job ? "

   " Yes, _____. "

   （A）I have it

   （B）I have one

   （C）I do

   （D）I certain have

   ＜解答＞ C（簡短回答）

432. " Mary, Can you tell me something about Jean ? "

   " Yes, Jean looked like her father, and she_____ after her mother in personality. "

   （A）acts

   （B）looks

   （C）runs

   （D）takes

   ＜解答＞ D（動詞）

433. " Why doesn't John take a trip overseas ? "

   " He has_____ money that he can't go abroad to travel. "

   （A）a little

   （B）such few

   （C）so little

   （D）such little

   ＜解答＞ C（形容詞）

434. " Do you ever go swimming ? "

" No, but I_____ like it very much. "

（A）am used to

（B）was used to

（C）use to

（D）used to

＜解答＞ D（動詞表示過去的習慣）

435. " Jackson succeeded. "

" I don't know_____ it. "

（A）how did he do

（B）how did he

（C）how did he it

（D）how he did

＜解答＞ D（名詞附屬子句）

436. " Johnson was late yesterday. "

" No wonder why I saw him_____. "

（A）run mad

（B）running mad

（C）running madly

（D）to run madly

＜解答＞ C（現在分詞+副詞）

437. " Mary, why did you go to the library ? "

" I went there_____ information. "

（A）for getting

（B）get

（C）to get

（D）got

＜解答＞ C（不定詞）

438. " Do you know Professor Baker ? "

" Of course, I do. I_____ him long ago in New York. "

（A）had met

（B）have met

（C）would meet

（D）met

＜解答＞ D（動詞一致性）

439.　" Why didn't you take that book with you ? "

" He said he_____ it for me. "

（A）was going

（B）taken

（C）had taken

（D）have taken

＜解答＞ C（動詞時態）

440.　" Why are you working so hard ? "

" This question is too difficult to work_____. "

（A）off

（B）up

（C）out

（D）through

＜解答＞ C（副詞）

441.　" What did your sister want you to do ? "

" My sister had me_____ that job all evening. "

（A）did

（B）do

（C）to do

（D）done

＜解答＞ B（沒有 to 的不定詞）

442.　" Why are you shouting so loudly ? "

" Because you cannot make_____ what I am saying. "

（A）out

（B）up

（C）over

（D）clear

　　＜解答＞　A（動詞片語）

443.　" What instructions did your boss give to you ? "

　　" He required that Alice＿＿＿ the meeting. "

　　（A）would attend

　　（B）attends

　　（C）attended

　　（D）attend

　　＜解答＞　D（假設語氣）

444.　" What happens in that new area ? "

　　" New houses＿＿＿ recently over there. "

　　（A）are built

　　（B）build

　　（C）have built

　　（D）have been built

　　＜解答＞　D（被動語態）

445.　" What does that house look like ? "

　　" That is similar in shape＿＿＿ that of mine. "

　　（A）with

　　（B）like

　　（C）as

　　（D）to

　　＜解答＞　D（介詞）

446.　" What did your teacher ask you to do a few days ago ? "

　　" She said she＿＿＿ punish me severely for my fault. "

　　（A）is going to

　　（B）will

　　（C）would

　　（D）was

　　＜解答＞　C（動詞時態）

447. " Are the children coming to visit you very soon ? "

" If they came, I_____ very happy. "

（A）would be

（B）will be

（C）would have been

（D）should have been

＜解答＞ A（條件句）

448. " If you want to plant good flower, you had better look up Botany_____. "

（A）third volume

（B）volume third

（C）the volume three

（D）the third volume

＜解答＞ D（序數形容詞）

449. " Oh, that's very strange but interesting. "

" I wasn't certain that he_____ to me about that. "

（A）would reveal

（B）reveals

（C）was revealing

（D）had revealed

＜解答＞ D（動詞時態）

450. " Did you go to see your aunt ? "

" No, but I_____. "

（A）might

（B）would

（C）could

（D）should have

＜解答＞ D（動詞）

451. " Do you think the news is true ? "

" Yes, _____. "

（A）I'm sure not it be true

（B）I'm not sure it to be true

（C）I'm sure it is true

（D）I'm not sure to be not true

＜解答＞　C（字序）

452.　" They don't seem to answer their phone. "

" There isn't anyone at home, ＿＿＿? "

（A）isn't there

（B）is there

（C）is it

（D）isn't it

＜解答＞　B（附加問題）

453.　" You look funny riding on bicycle. "

" Yes, I'm. I'm not＿＿＿ on bicycle. "

（A）use to riding

（B）used to ride

（C）to be used to riding

（D）used to riding

＜解答＞　D（動詞片語+動名詞表示現在的習慣）

454.　" Why do you look tired, John ? "

" The president had me＿＿＿ reports all afternoon. "

（A）to write

（B）written

（C）write

（D）wrote

＜解答＞　C（沒有 to 的不定詞）

455.　" I will call Mary, if you can tell me her phone number. "

" Wait a minute, I'll look it up on the＿＿＿. "

（A）phone's book

（B）phone book

（C）phones book

（D）book of phone

＜解答＞ B（名詞當形容詞用）

456. " I don't know I can ever find that book. "

" Did Professor Baker tell you how＿＿＿ find it there ? "

（A）can you

（B）could you

（C）you could

（D）would you

＜解答＞ C（字序）

457. " I just moved in here last Saturday. "

" Did you move in＿＿＿ with you ? "

（A）many furnitures

（B）much furnitures

（C）many furniture

（D）much furniture

＜解答＞ D（形容詞＋不可數名詞）

458. " Did you see Jean at the party last night ? "

" Jean is a very pretty girl. I＿＿＿ her if she had shown up. "

（A）would see

（B）had seen

（C）ought having seen

（D）should have seen

＜解答＞ D（條件句）

459. " How can I reach there very fast ? "

" You will get there＿＿＿ if you go by taxi. "

（A）more faster

（B）faster

（C）more fast

（D）more fastly

＜解答＞ B（比較）

460. " John, do you have a passport ? "

" No, but I wish I_____ one. "

（A）having

（B）have

（C）can have

（D）had

＜解答＞ D（假設語氣）

461. " I did go there. "

" What would you have done if you_____ to work yesterday ? "

（A）didn't have

（B）hadn't had

（C）didn't

（D）didn't have had

＜解答＞ B（條件句）

462. " Mr. Carpenter has been to the Caribbean several times. "

" He has done_____ business there. "

（A）a lot of

（B）a number of

（C）much

（D）lots

＜解答＞ A（形容詞）

463. " Is Miss Cook a good teacher ? "

" She would be a better teacher if she_____ so much. "

（A）talked

（B）didn't talk

（C）does talk

（D）had talked

＜解答＞ B（假設語氣）

464. " Do you like to go to the movies ? "

" Yes, _____ very much. "

（A）I like it

（B）I like

（C）I like them

（D）I like to

＜解答＞ C（代名詞）

465.　" Who are those boys ? "

"Those boys are friends of_____. "

（A）them

（B）they

（C）their

（D）theirs

＜解答＞ D（代名詞形式）

466.　" I don't like this pair. "

"What did Mr. Jack Marrow consider_____ for his nephew ? "

（A）buying

（B）to buy

（C）bought

（D）buy

＜解答＞ A（動名詞）

467.　" Oh, glad to see you, John. "

"What_____ you to the big city? Be here long ? "

（A）carries

（B）brings

（C）takes

（D）makes

＜解答＞ B（動詞）

468.　" Why did John kill it ? "

"I'll ask him why_____. "

（A）did he do it

（B）he did it

（C）he did

（D）does he do what

＜解答＞ C（名詞附屬子句）

469. " When did you go home? "

" As soon as I could, I_____ home. "

（A）go

（B）would go

（C）had gone

（D）went

＜解答＞ D（動詞一致性）

470. " Who should go to see him ? "

" I suggest that Mary_____ to see him. "

（A）go

（B）goes

（C）would go

（D）went

＜解答＞ A（沒有 to 的不定詞）

471. " What can I do ? "

" Please get the lawn_____. "

（A）to be mowed

（B）to mow

（C）mowing

（D）mowed

＜解答＞ D（過去分詞）

472. " If someone falls into deep water and can't swim, what will he be ? "

" _____ "

（A）drowing

（B）drown

（C）drowned

（D）the drowning

<解答> C（過去分詞）

473. " Where were the toys ? "

" The toys_____ in the box. "

（A）were

（B）putting

（C）might put

（D）put

<解答> A（動詞）

474. " Does he look out for trouble ? "

" He seldom looks out for trouble, _____. "

（A）does he

（B）hasn't he

（C）doesn't he

（D）won't he

<解答> A（附加問題）

475. " Hadn't you graduated from college ? "

" Yes, _____. "

（A）I study French for two years

（B）I am studying French for two years

（C）I studied French for two years

（D）I would study French for two years

<解答> C（主要子句）

476. " Charlie died yesterday. "

" He was such a good man that_____. "

（A）I have ever seen before

（B）I am ever seeing before

（C）I ever see before

（D）I had ever seen before

<解答> D（形容詞附屬子句）

477. " What should I do? "

" You have to kill them before you get_____ yourself. "

（A）to kill

（B）killing

（C）kill

（D）killed

＜解答＞　D（過去分詞）

478.　" Did you see the letter that I wrote yesterday ? "

" She saw the letter_____ here this morning. "

（A）laying

（B）lieing

（C）laid

（D）lying

＜解答＞　D（易混淆的字家族）

479.　" She is not interested in doing that. "

"_____. "

（A）She is not too

（B）She is not neither

（C）She is not either

（D）She doesn't either

＜解答＞　C（副詞）

480.　" Shall I wake you up tomorrow ? "

" Yes, _____. "

（A）please do

（B）you shall

（C）you will

（D）you may

＜解答＞　A（縮減的副詞子句）

481.　" What's the matter with her ? "

" She doesn't like the idea_____ to bed early. "

（A）on going

（B）to go

（C）in going

（D）of going

＜解答＞ D（修飾的片語）

482. " That man escaped. "

" He should have had his son_____ that man. "

（A）kill

（B）to kill

（C）to killing

（D）killing

＜解答＞ A（沒有 to 的不定詞）

483. " You should do your best to get good grades. "

" How high an average_____? "

（A）a scholarship student must maintain

（B）must a scholarship student maintain

（C）maintain a scholarship student

（D）student maintain his scholarship

＜解答＞ B（主詞和動詞位置）

484. " How can we measure the price and things ? "

" However much_____ it will be worth it. "

（A）it cost

（B）does it cost

（C）it costs

（D）costs it

＜解答＞ C（主詞和動詞位置）

485. " Who fought ? "

" The United States fought in_____. "

（A）the World II

（B）World War II

（C）Second World War

（D）the World War II

　　　＜解答＞　B（名詞+序數）

486.　" Does she have a daughter ? "

　　　" Yes, she has a＿＿＿ old daughter. "

　　（A）three-years

　　（B）three years

　　（C）three year

　　（D）three-year

　　　＜解答＞　D（名詞當形容詞用）

487.　" Shall we have something to eat ? "

　　　" Yes, let's have our waiter＿＿＿ some coffee. "

　　（A）bring

　　（B）to bring

　　（C）bringing

　　（D）brought

　　　＜解答＞　A（沒有 to 的不定詞）

488.　" Was Elliott happy ? "

　　　" Elliott found that he was really not＿＿＿ when his girl jilted him. "

　　（A）unhappy

　　（B）happily

　　（C）very happily

　　（D）unhappily

　　　＜解答＞　A（易混淆的字家族）

489.　" What did he buy ? "

　　　" Charlie bought＿＿＿. "

　　（A）two boxes of chalk

　　（B）two boxes chalks

　　（C）two boxes chalk

　　（D）two box chalk

　　　＜解答＞　A（數量的名詞+物質名詞）

490. " Where is the restaurant, Sir ? "

"The restaurant is right_____ the corner of Washington Street. "

（A）at

（B）of

（C）on

（D）in

＜解答＞ C（介詞）

491. "What seems to be the trouble ? "

" I feel a little_____. "

（A）tired

（B）tiring

（C）tire

（D）tires

＜解答＞ A（易混淆的字家族）

492. " What does he say ? "

" His words are_____. "

（A）humiliating

（B）very humiliate

（C）humiliated

（D）humiliate

＜解答＞ A（易混淆的字家族）

493. " Did you study English last night ? "

" We didn't study English last night, but we_____. "

（A）had studied

（B）could

（C）should

（D）could have

＜解答＞ D（動詞時態）

494. " How does he behave ? "

" He behaves himself_____. "

（A）well

（B）good

（C）nice

（D）kind

＜解答＞ A（副詞）

495. " When do you like to study ? "

" I like to study after the professor_____. "

（A）will arrive

（B）is arriving

（C）arrives

（D）arrived

＜解答＞ C（動詞一致性）

496. " How did she set her hair ? "

" She set her hair_____. "

（A）very lovely

（B）in curly

（C）curl

（D）curly

＜解答＞ B（修飾片語）

497. " When did you receive it ? "

" _____ received it a week before I left. "

（A）I'd

（B）I'm

（C）I

（D）I've

＜解答＞ C（主詞）

498. " I don't like the car. "

" If the car_____ no good, I would have to buy another one. "

（A）were

（B）is

（C）was

（D）are

<解答> A（假設語氣）

499. " How much is the new car ? "

" The new car costs more than a＿＿＿ car. "

（A）using

（B）used

（C）use

（D）never use

<解答> B（形容詞）

500. " Was the test hard ? "

" The test was so hard that he ＿＿＿ flunked it. "

（A）mostly

（B）most

（C）almost

（D）about

<解答> C（副詞）

501. " How did you hit the ball ? "

" We hit the ball＿＿＿. "

（A）hardly

（B）hard

（C）force

（D）quick

<解答> B（副詞－副詞和形容詞同形）

502. " Why did you explain it to her ? "

" I＿＿＿ it to her if I thought she would understand. "

（A）would explain

（B）will explain

（C）explain

（D）would have explained

<解答>　A（條件句）

503.　" Who did you talk to ? "

" I talked to the man_____ food. "

（A）sell

（B）sold

（C）selling

（D）selled

<解答>　C（易混淆的字家族）

504.　" How do you treat your aunt ? "

" _____ I go to see my aunt, I give her some money. "

（A）In case

（B）When

（C）Whenever

（D）The next time

<解答>　C（副詞附屬子句）

505.　" Charlie left a few days ago. "

" What time_____ ? "

（A）he returns home

（B）he returned home

（C）will he return home

（D）did he return home

<解答>　C（主詞和動詞位置）

506.　" What is the teacher doing now in the classroom ? "

" She is_____ a problem to the students. "

（A）asking

（B）talking

（C）describing

（D）explaining

<解答>　D（易混淆的字家族）

507.　" How can you get the answer ? "

" I could write the answers but I_____ no pen. "

（A）have had

（B）have

（C）had

（D）would have

＜解答＞ B（動詞）

508. " Is he going to there ? "

" I_____. "

（A）hope to be not

（B）don't hope it

（C）hope there

（D）hope not

＜解答＞ D（簡短回答）

509. " Does he know my address ? "

" He still doesn't know where_____. "

（A）you live

（B）do you live

（C）live you

（D）are you living

＜解答＞ A（字序）

510. " What are you doing with the babies ? "

" I want to stop the baby_____. "

（A）to cry

（B）from crying

（C）crying

（D）cried

＜解答＞ C（現在分詞）

511. " I was hurt there last night. "

" If I_____ been there, I could have helped you. "

（A）had

（B）have

（C）would have

（D）had had

<解答> A（條件句）

512. " What's the trouble ? "

" The family never agree about_____ shares of the property. "

（A）her

（B）its

（C）their

（D）his

<解答> C（代名詞形式）

513. " I never saw you before. "

" Can you recall_____ with me two years ago ? "

（A）staying

（B）to have stayed

（C）to stay

（D）having stayed

<解答> D（縮減的名詞子句）

514. " What is Mary ? "

" Was it_____ you were refering to ? "

（A）he

（B）they

（C）her

（D）she

<解答> C（代名詞形式）

515. " What do you need ? "

" Two pounds_____ all I need. "

（A）being

（B）is

（C）are

（D）have been

＜解答＞ B（動詞）

516. " Where is your money ? "

" My money was_____. "

（A）robbed

（B）lose

（C）not here no more

（D）stolen

＜解答＞D （被動語態）

517. I'll lend you the money _____.

（A）that you return it within six months

（B）and that you return it within six months

（C）you return it within six months

（D）on condition that you return it within six months

＜解答＞ D（連接詞）

518. " The table is broken. "

" Then it needs_____. "

（A）be fixed

（B）fix

（C）fixing

（D）to fix

＜解答＞ C（動名詞）

519. " What can you do ? "

" We can do nothing unless she_____ happy tomorrow. "

（A）will be

（B）is

（C）shall be

（D）were

＜解答＞ B（動詞）

520. " I'm hungry, and I want to eat this bread. "

" Wait ! It is not good_____. "

（A）for eating

（B）to be eaten

（C）to eat

（D）eating

<解答>　C（不定詞）

521.　" Why is she unhappy ? "

" She_____ cook the beef. "

（A）can't

（B）doesn't have to

（C）wasn't able

（D）can not to

<解答>　A（助動詞）

522.　" I bought that book anyway. "

" If I had money, I_____ that. "

（A）wouldn't have bought

（B）won't buy

（C）shan't buy

（D）wouldn't buy

<解答>　D（假設語氣）

523.　" You didn't go to the party, did you ? "

" I do wish I_____ there. "

（A）was

（B）were

（C）had been

（D）went

<解答>　C（假設語氣）

524.　" Did he stop walking at last ? "

" No, he kept_____ there. "

（A）go

（B）to go

（C）going

（D）from going

　　＜解答＞　C（動名詞）

525.　" Who knows the way ? "

　　" He knows the way_____. "

　　（A）to go

　　（B）going

　　（C）goes

　　（D）is going

　　＜解答＞　A（不定詞）

526.　" What does her mother do ? "

　　" Her mother asks her children_____ the truth. "

　　（A）telling

　　（B）tell

　　（C）to tell

　　（D）have to tell

　　＜解答＞　C（不定詞）

527.　" Do you want to go with me ? "

　　" No, I_____. "

　　（A）would rather not

　　（B）hadn't rather

　　（C）had rather stay

　　（D）would not rather

　　＜解答＞　A（簡短回答＋字序）

528.　" What happens ? "

　　" The situation is_____. "

　　（A）embarrassed

　　（B）embarrass

　　（C）embarrassing

（D）very much embarrassed

<解答> C（易混淆的字家族）

529. " He had a great deal of trouble with _____. "

" What was he angry for ? "

（A）the store's management

（B）the stores management

（C）the management of the store

（D）store's management

<解答> C（名詞片語）

530. " My English isn't good. "

" How many years ago_____ English ? "

（A）did you study

（B）had you studied

（C）have you studied

（D）do you study

<解答> A（主詞和動詞的位置）

531. " Can you have dinner with me tonight ? "

" No, but I_____ to have dinner with your father. "

（A）had like

（B）will like

（C）like

（D）would like

<解答> D（動詞）

532. " Who rode faster ? "

" That girl in white rode more slowly on the highway_____ this boy. "

（A）as

（B）like

（C）with

（D）than

<解答> D（比較）

533. " I have to go under any circumstances. "

" If you do follow my advice, I _____ you. "

（A）don't punish

（B）wouldn't punish

（C）would not to punish

（D）won't punish

＜解答＞ D（條件句）

534. " Who's got all my money ? "

" I_____. "

（A）do

（B）have

（C）am

（D）got

＜解答＞ B（簡短回答）

535. " The cake is delicious, John. "

" Then, do you want_____ more ? "

（A）a little

（B）some

（C）little

（D）much

＜解答＞ B（代名詞）

536. " What does your aunt act ? "

" She ascts as though she_____ an expert. "

（A）has been

（B）is

（C）was

（D）were

＜解答＞ D（假設語氣）

537. " I didn't do it. "

" He insisted that you_____ it. "

（A）would do

（B）had done

（C）did

（D）had to do

＜解答＞ B（動詞時態）

538. " What do you think about English ? "

" It's a difficult language_____. "

（A）speaking

（B）speak

（C）to speak

（D）spoke

＜解答＞ C（不定詞）

539. " What did they struggle for ? "

" The two men resisted_____ it. "

（A）to examine

（B）examining

（C）by examine

（D）examine

＜解答＞ B（現在分詞）

540. " What can he do ? "

" I_____ that he follow my advice. "

（A）suggest

（B）hope

（C）believe

（D）wish

＜解答＞ A（動詞）

541. " Who talked to you ? "

" My sister whispered_____ my ear. "

（A）in

（B）to

（C）with

（D）on

＜解答＞ A（介詞）

542. " Did she ? "

" Mary_____ to the climate of Chicago. "

（A）is used

（B）used to

（C）uses

（D）use to

＜解答＞ A（動詞片語）

543. " Shall we go now ? "

" I wonder what_____. "

（A）time it is

（B）time is it

（C）it is time

（D）is time

＜解答＞ A（名詞附屬子句）

544. " What did you hear ? "

" We heard_____ long lecture that we were falling asleep. "

（A）such a

（B）too

（C）so

（D）such

＜解答＞ A（形容詞）

545. " Oh! I'll go travelling. "

" It is_____ warm weather that the roses will bloom. "

（A）so

（B）such

（C）so a

（D）very

<解答>　B（形容詞）

546.　" Where should I get my tickets ? "

　　　" You＿＿＿ your tickets last month. "

　　　（A）should get

　　　（B）should have gotten

　　　（C）had got

　　　（D）ought to get

　　　<解答>　B（動詞）

547.　" He would go to see you. "

　　　" ＿＿＿ he did not come ? "

　　　（A）What if

　　　（B）Where if

　　　（C）What come

　　　（D）Why whether

　　　<解答>　A（代名詞）

548.　" Is Peter a good student ? "

　　　" Yes, but he has no＿＿＿ in Algebra. "

　　　（A）interesting

　　　（B）interested

　　　（C）interest

　　　（D）study

　　　<解答>　C（名詞）

549.　" Do you want the pants ? "

　　　" My pants＿＿＿ laid in bed. "

　　　（A）is

　　　（B）was

　　　（C）are

　　　（D）being

　　　<解答>　C（動詞一致性）

550.　" What can I do for you ? "

" Do You_____ John open them? "

（A）permit

（B）allow

（C）let

（D）need

＜解答＞　C（動詞）

551.　_____ his research was inconclusive, Dr. John Smith continued to experiment with it.

（A）Although

（B）Unless

（C）Until

（D）Because

＜解答＞　D（連接詞）

552.　The costs of college　　　　　.

（A）increase each year

（B）go higher per year

（C）are flying high every year

（D）boom high in every year

＜解答＞　A（動詞）

553.　_____ also occurred in the suburbs.

（A）Students and their demonstrations

（B）Students with their demonstrations

（C）Students in their demonstrations

（D）Students demonstrations

＜解答＞　D（主詞）

554.　_____ settlement of this problem without first looking into its causes.

（A）There is not

（B）There must be not

（C）There can be no

（D）It is no

<解答>　C（主詞和動詞的位置）

555. Criticism of the president of the company became less and less serious until_____.

　　（A）it ceased altogether

　　（B）it finished finally

　　（C）it stopped entirely itself

　　（D）it concluded itself

　　<解答>　A（副詞附屬子句）

556. The area between the bay and the airport will be the best place_____.

　　（A）for the future tourist development

　　（B）that can be developed for tourists in the future

　　（C）around town for the future expanding tourism

　　（D）to have the tourist industry in the future

　　<解答>　A（形容詞片語）

557. After four days of debate that_____ until dawn, the parliament unanimously approved the construction.

　　（A）have often lasted

　　（B）has often lasted

　　（C）often lasted

　　（D）often lasts

　　<解答>　C（副詞和動詞的位置）

558. Only by doing the work themselves_____.

　　（A）the students will get experience

　　（B）the students will gets experience

　　（C）will the students get experience

　　（D）will the students to get experience

　　<解答>　C（倒裝句）

559. Her child was born_____.

　　（A）it's five years

　　（B）for five years

（C）since five year

（D）five years ago

＜解答＞ D（副詞片語）

560. We can go to a restaurant or eat at home, _____.

（A）whichever you prefer

（B）why ever you want

（C）however you do

（D）wherever you go

＜解答＞ A（副詞附屬子句）

561. _____ that a decision in the case may be difficult.

（A）As mentioned before

（B）Mentioned before is

（C）It has been mentioned before

（D）Mentioned it was before

＜解答＞ C（ it.....that 的構句）

562. _____ about the administrative changes suggested.

（A）There is much to be said

（B）To be said will be many

（C）For it can be said

（D）Said it can be a lot

＜解答＞ A（主詞和動詞的位置）

563. _____ was the result of many years of hard work.

（A）Acted by superb Charlie Chaplin

（B）Charlie Chaplin's superb acting

（C）Acting superbly of Charlie Chaplin's

（D）Charlie Chaplin acted superbly

＜解答＞ B（名詞片語）

564. Bill had heart attack_____ his new job.

（A）just before he was to take

（B）before he had just taking

（C）before he was just taking

（D）just before he has to take

<解答> A（副詞附屬子句）

565.　_____ that Richard could not come, Doris would never have given the party.

（A）She had known

（B）Had she known

（C）Did she know

（D）She did known

<解答> B（倒裝句）

566.　Both of the Mayor's speeches on education were good, but the second was plainly the_____.

（A）best of the two

（B）best of both

（C）better of the two

（D）better of each

<解答> C（比較）

567.　Take an umbrella when you go to Seattle, for it rains_____ there.

（A）frequently

（B）as frequent

（C）most of times

（D）much time

<解答> A（副詞）

568.　If I had hurried, I_____ the train.

（A）would catch

（B）could catch

（C）would have caught

（D）had caught

<解答> C（條件句）

569.　My coat looks rather shabby, so I ought to have it_____.

（A）clean and press

（B）cleaning and pressing

（C）cleaned and pressed

（D）cleaning and pressed

＜解答＞ C（過去分詞）

570. I would have told him the answer had it been possible, but I＿＿＿ so busy then.

（A）had been

（B）were

（C）was

（D）would be

＜解答＞ C（動詞時態）

571. My hair style is not in vague, but I am used to＿＿＿ my hair long.

（A）having

（B）wearing

（C）growing

（D）reserning

＜解答＞ B（動名詞）

572. I like black coffee so much because the stronger it is, ＿＿＿.

（A）I like it better

（B）the more I like

（C）the better I like it

（D）I like it more

＜解答＞ C（平行構句）

573. ＿＿＿ the drought in Kansas has become less serious.

（A）It is apparently that

（B）It appears that

（C）It must have been that

（D）There is appearance that

＜解答＞ B（ it.....that 構句）

574. I have never been to Rome but that's the city＿＿＿.

(A) where I most like to visit

(B) I'd most like to visit

(C) which I like to visit most

(D) what I'd like most to visit

＜解答＞ B（形容詞附屬子句）

575. Children learn very quickly. When they learn about a new subject they often_____.

(A) become too interested

(B) very much are interested

(C) become much interested

(D) are interested very much

＜解答＞ C（主要子句）

576. John has a new car. I wonder when_____ it.

(A) he got

(B) did her get

(C) he gets

(D) he is getting

＜解答＞ A（名詞附屬子句）

577. Helen couldn't go to France after all. That's too bad, I'm sure she would have enjoyed it if_____.

(A) she's gone

(B) se'll go

(C) she'd gone

(D) she'd go

＜解答＞ C（條件句）

578. The meeting was put off because we_____ a meeting without John.

(A) are objected to have

(B) were objected to having

(C) objected to have

(D) objected to having

<解答>　D（副詞子句）

579.　Have you seen Henry lately? My boss wants to know_____.

　　（A）how is he getting along

　　（B）how he is getting along

　　（C）what is he getting along

　　（D）waht he is getting along

　　<解答>　B（名詞附屬子句）

580.　In 1890 there were many American cities and towns where part of a day's

　　school instruction was conducted in languages_____ English.

　　（A）more than

　　（B）except

　　（C）other than

　　（D）except for

　　<解答>　C（副詞）

581.　Many farmers built silos_____ to store grains.

　　（A）with which

　　（B）which

　　（C）in which

　　（D）in there

　　<解答>　C（修飾片詞）

582.　Juditch won't be rehearsing with us today and_____.

　　（A）Maurice won't too

　　（B）so won't Maurice

　　（C）neither will Maurice

　　（D）either won't Maurice

　　<解答>　C（主詞和動詞的位置）

583.　Anna said in her letter that she'd appreciate_____ from you some time.

　　（A）to hear

　　（B）having heard

　　（C）hearing

（D）to hearing

<解答> C（動名詞）

584. Jane has brown hair in fact, it's quite similar in shade_____ yours.

（A）as

（B）with

（C）like

（D）to

<解答> D（介詞）

585. My father likes to play golf; he's really enthusiastic_____ it.

（A）by

（B）about

（C）with

（D）on

<解答> B（介詞）

586. Who's that good-looking girl Frank's dancing with? I_____ her before.

（A）never had seen

（B）had never seen

（C）was never seeing

（D）never saw

<解答> D（動詞時態）

587. Is there anything you want from town? I am going to get_____.

（A）those letters mailed

（B）mailed letters

（C）to mail those letters

（D）those letters mail

<解答> A（過去分詞）

588. I have enjoyed my visit here. I'll be very sorry_____.

（A）for leaving

（B）of leaving

（C）to leave

（D）with leaving

＜解答＞ C（不定詞）

589. Have you been to the science museum lately ? I_____.

（A）last went on Thursday there

（B）went there last Thursday

（C）went last there on Thursday

（D）went on last there Thursday

＜解答＞ B（動詞和副詞的位置）

590. John isn't a diligetn student, for it is the third time he has been late, _____?

（A）wasn't

（B）hasn't it

（C）isn't it

（D）has it

＜解答＞ C（附加問題）

591. You didn't hear us come in last night. That's good. We tried_____ noisy.

（A）to be not

（B）not to be

（C）not be

（D）be not

＜解答＞ B（否定的不定詞）

592. Mr. Smith looks very happy today. He has got_____ good news from home.

（A）many

（B）much

（C）quite a few

（D）a few

＜解答＞ B（形容詞）

593. Have you finished your homework? This lesson is_____ than the last one.

（A）more easier

（B）more easy

（C）very easier

（D）much easier

<解答>　D（比較）

594.　John may win the first prize. He has started_____ the speed of 80 miles.

（A）at

（B）of

（C）on

（D）in

<解答>　A（介詞）

595.　I didn't help him. I would have_____ I didn't have the money then.

（A）or

（B）but

（C）otherwise

（D）still

<解答>　B（連接詞）

596.　What did he say in the letter? I really can't_____ it out.

（A）make

（B）put

（C）run

（D）come

<解答>　A（動詞片語）

597.　How will it turn out? Well, it all_____.

（A）depends on

（B）is depending

（C）depends

（D）depend

<解答>　C（動詞）

598.　At the City University this year_____ are enrolled in special seminars in writing for radio and television.

（A）more students are before ever

（B）many students than before ever

（C）more students than ever before

（D）many students are ever before

<解答> C（比較）

599. Martin visited his aunt two days before he_____ town.

（A）left

（B）will leave

（C）had left

（D）is going to leave

<解答> A（動詞時態）

600. I'm not going to ask the teacher why he gave me that grade; I intend_____.

（A）to let rest the matter

（B）the matter to be let resting

（C）letting the matter to rest

（D）to let the matter rest

<解答> D（不定詞）

601. Mr. Gilmore has a strange disease, but the doctor's hope to fine_____.

（A）a cure

（B）curing

（C）for it a cure

（D）a curing

<解答> A（冠詞+名詞）

602. Edward like classical music and I think that he prefers it_____ any other kind.

（A）than

（B）over

（C）to

（D）against

<解答> C（比較）

603. I enjoyed the movie very much. I wish I_____ the book from which it was made.

（A）have read

（B）had read

（C）should have read

（D）am reading

＜解答＞ B（假設語氣）

604. They don't seem to answer their phone when I call; there isn't anyone at home, _____?

（A）isn't there

（B）is there

（C）is it

（D）isn't it

＜解答＞ B（附加問題）

605. All the people in this village have black hair; they all_____ each other.

（A）resemble as

（B）resemble with

（C）resemble

（D）resemble from

＜解答＞ C（動詞）

606. His eyes are blue as_____.

（A）the sun shines in the sky

（B）a Scandinavion

（C）a Scandinavian's

（D）German

＜解答＞ C（所有格）

607. A person who is not an expert should never eat mushrooms gathered in the woods, _____.

（A）for you may be seriously poisoned if you do

（B）for he may be seriously poisoned if you do

（C）for they will be certainly poisoned if they do

（D）for he may be seriously poisoned if he does

<解答>　D（副詞附屬子句）

608. Jean had not realized how long the magazine was or_____.

　（A）its reading difficulty

　（B）that it was so difficult to read

　（C）its difficulty in reading

　（D）how difficult it was to read

　<解答>　D（平行構句）

609. He liked swimming and_____.

　（A）go hiking

　（B）taking long hikes

　（C）to take long hikes

　（D）went to hike

　<解答>　B（平行構句）

610. In making preparation for the experiment, _____.

　（A）thorough washing of all glassware is advised for the students

　（B）the students should wash all glassware thoroughly

　（C）all glassware should be thoroughly washed

　（D）wahing thoroughly of all the glassware is advised

　<解答>　B（主要子句）

611. One of the laboratory mice was frightened and bit back_____.

　（A）giving Dr. Tagram a scratch that became infected and caused death

　（B）frighten the old scientist eye for eye

　（C）with its long paws and tail to attack the old scientist

　（D）making a loud harsh voice commanding Dr. Tagram stop his pursuing

　<解答>　A（形容詞附屬子句）

612. John is firmly persuaded_____.

　（A）of his wife's innocence

　（B）in his insistence

　（C）as if he was reght

　（D）on his committing the crimes

<解答> A（修飾片語）

613. The English is a heterogeneous and contradistory race_____.

    （A）with acting direction

    （B）with conservative tendencies

    （C）in a direction unable to follow

    （D）being actively pursued

    <解答> B（修飾片語）

614. A certain type of board is sold only in lengths_____.

    （A）in multiple 3 by feet

    （B）of mutiples of 2 feet from 6 ft. to 24 ft.

    （C）by multiples of everything

    （D）which can have no multiples

    <解答> B（修飾片語）

615. Most factory acts passed in England during the first half of the nineteenth century were sponsored by the_____.

    （A）Tory Party wanted to create economic diffculties for the factory owners who controlled the Whig Party

    （B）Whig Party represented the interests of the downtrodden

    （C）Anglican Church which at that time sought to extend its influence over England's rapidly growing laboring class

    （D）Labor Party which consisted large of factory workers

    <解答> C（形容詞附屬子句）

616. My weekend plans were upset by a surprise_____.

    （A）visit from my uncle and aunt

    （B）travel from my uncle and aunt

    （C）incident from my uncle and aunt

    （D）visitation from my uncle and aunt

    <解答> A（形容詞附屬子句）

617. In removing the stripped bolt_____.

    （A）a hacksaw is used intensively

（B）the mechanic had to use a hacksaw

（C）a hacksaw had to be used by the mechanic

（D）it was found that the mechanic would have to use a hacksaw

＜解答＞ B（主詞和動詞的位置）

618. We certainly have no objection to_____.

（A）be one of members of the party

（B）have to read such an uninteresting story

（C）go to see Mr. Williams

（D）giving him that chance

＜解答＞ D（動名詞）

619. Dick was an excellent English teacher and_____.

（A）an outstanding orator

（B）who was an outstanding orator

（C）was superior at giving speeches

（D）made good speeches

＜解答＞ A（名詞片語）

620. We hear of the educational value of exhibitions of stuffed birds and it may be conceded that_____.

（A）it might be made useful

（B）they might be made of use

（C）they might be made very useful

（D）these exhibitions might be made useful

＜解答＞ D（名詞附屬子句）

621. The pen_____.

（A）was laying on the table, where it had laid all week

（B）was lying on the table, where it had laid all week

（C）was laying on the table, where it had been laid all week

（D）was lying on the table, where it had been laid all week

＜解答＞ D（動詞+語氣）

622. Julie speaks English as though_____.

（A）she were an American

（B）he is an American

（C）he was an American

（D）he were an American

＜解答＞ A（假設語氣）

623. The gentleman was apparently content_____.

（A）to patiently wait outside the door

（B）to wait outside patiently the door

（C）wait patiently outside the door

（D）to wait outside the door patiently

＜解答＞ D（形容詞和副詞的位置）

624. According to this paragraph, _____.

（A）John has hurry every morning

（B）his father had to cut out smoke

（C）they have four kid now

（D）his papAdidn't mind to be janitor

＜解答＞ A（主詞和動詞的位置）

625. Caruco turned away from the horn_____.

（A）as if he is very happy

（B）if he had been happy

（C）like what he did before

（D）as he finished singing the last note

＜解答＞ D（副詞附屬子句）

626. According to what he told me, _____.

（A）after it had lain in the rain all night, it is not fit for use again

（B）they will have gone before the notice sent to their office

（C）we will send Acopy of the article for you if you wish it

（D）I will not go unless I receive a special invitation

＜解答＞ D（主詞和動詞的位置）

627. The day I was supposed to leave, _____.

（A）I realize I still haven't received my passport and visa

（B）I had no idea how much was there going to do

（C）I simply couldn't believe the time had passed so qucikly

（D）I had no idea how much there is to do and I waited too long before I began getting ready

＜解答＞ C（主要子句）

628. Foods are classified with respect to their power to yield energy, to build tissue, and_____.

（A）their ability to regulate body processes

（B）to regulate body processes for their ability is required

（C）able to regulate body processes

（D）to regulate body processes

＜解答＞ D（平行構句）

629. If you stay over four years in the United States, you will have to_____.

（A）extending your visAto a certain time of your stay

（B）have your visa extended to one more year

（C）extending your visa one year longer

（D）have one year's extension

＜解答＞ B（條件句）

630. Do not try setting grantie slabs in ordinary concrete, and_____.

（A）not do anything wrong

（B）instead use a thick plaster of Paris

（C）you should instead use a thick plaster of Paris

（D）you must use some other concrete

＜解答＞ B（平行構句）

631. We will not allow them to rent until_____.

（A）they will have finished the work

（B）they have his work finish

（C）they would have had their work finished

（D）they have finished the work

<解答> D（副詞附屬子句）

632. In this region it rains_____.

 （A）in the greatest amount of time

 （B）almost all of the time

 （C）in the large of the time

 （D）during the bulk of the time

 <解答> B（副詞片語）

633. He wanted to make his son receive a good education, travel extensively, and_____.

 （A）enjoy many other advantages

 （B）many other advantages are shared by him

 （C）to other advantages are many more

 （D）many other advantages

 <解答> A（平行構句）

634. To the discontent expressed by others, he_____.

 （A）paid deafness to them

 （B）paid no heed to them

 （C）turned a deaf ear

 （D）turned his back to

 <解答> C（動詞）

635. Those who violate the rules_____.

 （A）should meet severe punishment

 （B）must be severely punished

 （C）must be punished severe

 （D）should have punishment

 <解答> B（被動語態）

636. The speech is man's inheritance and the one that_____.

 （A）mark him different from animal

 （B）prevents him differently from animal

 （C）distinguishes him from animal

（D）identifies him from animal

<解答> C（形容詞附屬子句）

637. While in grammar school, _____.

（A）my father gave me a watch

（B）a watch was given to me by my father

（C）I was glad to have possessed a new bicycle

（D）my proudest possession was a new car

<解答> C（主詞和動詞的位置）

638. As a rule, most people are more or less resolute_____.

（A）to abopt a new idea

（B）to bring the justice with him

（C）on taking a new thoutht

（D）in accepting an invitation

<解答> D（修飾片語）

639. I do deeply believe that_____

（A）people are apt to be sued for breach of contract

（B）people are liable to be lazy

（C）most of our pilgrim fathers located in Pennsylvania

（D）the words apt and likely are often interchanged

<解答> D（名詞附屬子句）

640. Is it true that_____?

（A）Tenth Street, at the end of whose he lives

（B）you didn't come on account of you didn't get your invitation

（C）you have no other samples except these to show me

（D）you spent most of your time outdoors

<解答> D（副詞附屬子句）

641. Paul was the salesman who turned in the most orders and_____.

（A）to win the company contest

（B）winner of the company contest

（C）winning the company contest

（D）won the company contest

＜解答＞　D（動詞一致性）

642.　Under such circumstances, _____.

（A）I had to act as disinterested observer in these negotiations

（B）I had to dissent with the religion in which I had been born

（C）I had to confide my friends

（D）we had to broke the chair

＜解答＞　A（主詞和動詞的位置）

643.　My uncle says that_____.

（A）my aunt sat her suitcase in a corner

（B）he rises at five o'clock every morning

（C）the river had raised two feet during the night

（D）from where he was lying, he could see a small black box setting on the table

＜解答＞　B（名詞附屬子句）

644.　It is said that_____.

（A）for six months the factory machinery has laid idle

（B）I finished laying the bricks, but they did not lay evenly

（C）my mother immediately set the kettle on the stove

（D）we must have set three hours waiting for him

＜解答＞　D（名詞附屬子句）

645.　An incessant destruction individuls must have been going on through their being swept up the beaches and dried, or_____.

（A）they wouldn't be able be reach the sea

（B）it was swept out

（C）by their being swept out to sea and sinking down out of air and sun

（D）he wouldn't go down to the sea

＜解答＞　C（平行構句）

646.　Jean wanted neither the assignment in Tokyo nor_____.

（A）the job in Chicago

（B）did she want to go to Chicago

（C）to be sent to Chicago

（D）at Chicago

　　＜解答＞　A（連接詞一致性）

647. Over this world of barren rock_____.

　　（A）there were great changes of climate

　　（B）a climate can sustain without changes

　　（C）a climate is being changed

　　（D）changing climate seems radical

　　＜解答＞　A（主詞和動詞的位置）

648. As a matter of fact, I have lost_____.

　　（A）the greatest amount of money

　　（B）the large share of the money

　　（C）almost all my money

　　（D）a considerable sum of money

　　＜解答＞　D（形容詞）

649. To the opinions given by all his friends, he_____.

　　（A）appreciate them very much

　　（B）did not value them at all

　　（C）didn't accept

　　（D）paid no attention

　　＜解答＞　D（動詞）

650. We must accomplish this job to the_____.

　　（A）highest profit

　　（B）fullest benefit

　　（C）greatest adventage

　　（D）most advantageous increase

　　＜解答＞　B（形容詞）

651. The silence was broken by the clash of the garden gate, a tap at the door, and_____.

（A）the door is opened

（B）is opened

（C）being opened

（D）its opening

<解答> D（名詞片語）

652. Let us not be afraid_____.

（A）to finish when we have attained the end

（B）to end when we have achieved the end

（C）of ending when the end has been completed

（D）to end when we have reached the end

<解答> D（不定詞+副詞子句）

653. All factors considered, the opinion that the net cost of goods produced will be_____.

（A）many higher

（B）lowest

（C）about same

（D）somewhat higher

<解答> D（形容詞）

654. Toward morning they found themselves unable to feed the fire, _____.

（A）which died down by and by

（B）that died off gradually

（C）which being extinguished

（D）which gradually died away

<解答> D（形容詞附屬子句）

655. Before, I criticize this rule_____.

（A）tribute to its enduring importance is to be made

（B）its enduring importance should be regarded tribute

（C）I must pay tribute to its enduring importance

（D）we must take tribute to the enduring importance

<解答> C（主要子句）

656. General James Jones will contribute not only his time but also_____.

 （A）will be give up his property to this country

 （B）help building his country

 （C）his property to his country

 （D）he will help his country to be built

 ＜解答＞ C（連接詞一致性）

657. While traveling through the Blue Ridge Mountains, _____.

 （A）the breath-taking scenes attracted the travelers

 （B）the scenes attracted the travelers deeply

 （C）the travelers attracted the scenes

 （D）the travelers were awed by the breath-taking scenes

 ＜解答＞ D（主詞和動詞的位置）

658. His career has been an active one_____.

 （A）writing poetry, working on magazines, and the war in Greece

 （B）poetry, editing magazines, and the Greek war

 （C）writing poems, editing magazines, and serving in the Greek war

 （D）poetry work, editing magazines, and fighting in Greece

 ＜解答＞ C（平行構句）

659. Around the hemisphere, the general reaction to the speech was_____.

 （A）almost disadvantageous like himself

 （B）most favorable as his

 （C）almost as favorable as Ambassador Margain

 （D）almost as good as hers

 ＜解答＞ D（副詞位置）

660. The author wrote a pleasant story that is_____.

 （A）gay, but not entirely frivolous

 （B）more gay and still has not just frivolity

 （C）gay while not just giving frivolty to it

 （D）gay, but without giving only a frivolous treatment

 ＜解答＞ A（形容詞附屬子句）

661. Evidence was given on both sides of the issue but most of the facts_____.

    （A）stuck with the speaker's poing of view

    （B）gave the speaker's argument

    （C）supported the speaker's position

    （D）witnessed the point of view of the speaker

    ＜解答＞ C（動詞）

662. Because of the standardization of people and products_____.

    （A）there is much reson that our time is known as the Age of Conformity

    （B）our age can justly be called the Age of Conformity

    （C）for many reasons this time is noted as the Age of Conformity

    （D）the Age of Conformity is what our time is know by

    ＜解答＞ B（主詞和動詞的位置）

663. In 1929 the country suffered a period of economic depression_____.

    （A）unlike anything it had ever experienced before

    （B）and was the likes of which it had never witnessed before

    （C）and before it had never had this

    （D）while before the likes of this depression had not been

    ＜解答＞ A（副詞附屬子句）

664. Although their strengths lie in different areas, the two nations_____.

    （A）are quite equal in totalness of power

    （B）have a total that is equal in power

    （C）are approximately equal in power

    （D）share in total an equality of power

    ＜解答＞ C（避免冗長）

665. To finance the program they had to turn to_____.

    （A）the public in the way of raising money

    （B）fund raising for money of the public

    （C）appealing money from the public

    （D）the public for the funds they needed

    ＜解答＞ D（名詞子句）

666. Among the advantages which Mr. Barlow has given his children are a good college education and_____.

 (A) extensive travel abroad

 (B) to travel extensively abroad

 (C) travel extensively abroad

 (D) of extensive traveling abroad

 ＜解答＞ A（連接詞一致性）

667. To the liberally educated mind, the first duty is_____.

 (A) to combine the ideas that appear unrelated

 (B) to compound the ideas that are different

 (C) to unite into one thing the unrelated ideas

 (D) to join the unrelated ideas together

 ＜解答＞ D（簡化）

668. After thinking about it for a long time, he finally decided   .

 (A) to under take the task

 (B) to make such a task

 (C) to commit the task

 (D) to endeavor the task

 ＜解答＞ A（不定詞）

669. From all accounts the king was greatly loved by his friends, respected by his subjects, and_____.

 (A) his enemies deared him

 (B) feared by his enemies

 (C) he scared his enemies

 (D) frightened his enemies

 ＜解答＞ B（平行構句）

670. The higher court reversed the decision of the lower court because the order_____.

 (A) infringed on the right of the accused

 (B) restrained the rights of accused

(C) took the rights of the accused

(D) infringed the accused of his rights

<解答> A (副詞附屬子句)

671. Nineteen people were already dead, _____.

(A) seven of them were teenagers

(B) seven being teenagers

(C) teenagers were seven

(D) among seven were teenagers

<解答> B (簡化)

672. James liked fishing_____.

(A) but hunting had been also enjoyed by him

(B) but hunting was also enjoyed by him

(C) but hunting was also enjoyed

(D) but he also enjoyed hunting

<解答> D (連接詞一致性)

673. Arthur was remembered as a talented musician_____.

(A) and a skilled painter as well

(B) and as painting skillfully

(C) thus his skill as a painter

(D) in addition to skillful painting

<解答> A (連接詞一致性)

674. Many of these costumes for the play are torn_____.

(A) and mending is required of them

(B) but need mending

(C) but require of be mended

(D) and need to be mended

<解答> D (被動語態)

675. My grandfather has decided to make me go back to college immediately, study my lessons carefully, and_____.

(A) a master's degree must be attained

（B）must attain my master's degree

（C）attain my master's degree

（D）to my master's degree I have to attain

＜解答＞ C（連接詞一致性）

676. After finishing his work, John decided to＿＿＿.

（A）attain his success in drawing pictures

（B）achieve success in picture drawn

（C）draw pictures by success

（D）go on with his amateurish attempt to draw pictures

＜解答＞ D（不定詞）

677. Because man is a gregarious animal＿＿＿.

（A）he has no time to be with others

（B）other animals are unlike him

（C）he enjoys the companionship of others

（D）all animals need companionship

＜解答＞ C（主要子句）

678. Hunger, cold, and sickness were among the hardships of pioneer life＿＿＿.

（A）but life is short

（B）but, in the end, they overcame them

（C）and they experienced hardships

（D）therefore they did not enduce

＜解答＞ B（副詞附屬子句）

679. A scientific man must expect disappointments and injustices＿＿＿.

（A）otherwise he will succesd

（B）unless he succeeds

（C）in order to succeed

（D）if he is succeed

＜解答＞ C（介詞片語）

680. In his lecture this morning, Professor Baker explained＿＿＿.

（A）both the cause of the war and what its result was

（B）both what was the cause and what was its results

（C）both the cause of the war and its results

（D）both the cause and the result of the war

　　＜解答＞ D（連接詞一致性）

681. The hotel has a bar for the people＿＿＿＿.

（A）and can drink there

（B）and can eat there

（C）and drinking there in it

（D）and a cafeteria for dinner

　　＜解答＞ D（連接詞一致性）

682. That assistant professor rechecked the data available, ＿＿＿＿.

（A）and the report was corrected

（B）and they corrected the first report

（C）and he corrected the first report

（D）but the report was not corrected

　　＜解答＞ C（連接詞形式）

683. Associated with his characteristic, he is a(n)＿＿＿＿.

（A）aristocratic American

（B）high class American

（C）upper-class American

（D）inherited American

　　＜解答＞ C（名詞片語）

684. On enough logical reasons, the fewer seeds, ＿＿＿＿.

（A）the less plants grow

（B）the fewer plants

（C）the less plants

（D）the plants the fewer

　　＜解答＞ B（平行構句）

685. I would like to say that＿＿＿＿.

（A）if a child want to lie on the street, let him do it

（B）let him lay on the street if a child wants to lie on the ground

（C）if your children want to lie on the ground, let them do what he wants to do

（D）if he wants to lie on the street, let him do what he would like to do

＜解答＞ D（名詞附屬子句）

686. It is true that_____.

（A）he needs a teacher who cannot read

（B）he cannot read and he needs a teacher

（C）he needs a techer and he cannot read

（D）he who cannot read, needs a teacher

＜解答＞ D（字序）

687. Since the war our country has taken many important steps_____.

（A）to release its financial difficulties

（B）to improve its economic situation

（C）to ascend its financial standing

（D）to achieve its economical betterment

＜解答＞ B（不定詞）

688. Only in the relative calm late in the week could_____.

（A）a real count be taken of the devastation

（B）sick she might be

（C）he is happy to do that

（D）she became sick

＜解答＞ A（倒裝句）

689. In the nether would of the narcotics addict, _____.

（A）loyal is to man himself

（B）man loyalty is to himself

（C）man ambition is to herself

（D）a man's only loyalty is to himself

＜解答＞ D（主詞和動詞的位置）

690. Soviet Russia sent many diplomatic delegates to participate in a conference of some nature in Geneva, but no one said_____.

　　（A）what should be say

　　（B）what should be said

　　（C）what they should have said

　　（D）what be should have said

　　＜解答＞　D（名詞附屬子句）

691. Because we were unfamiliar with the route, _____.

　　（A）we decided to ask for advice due to the approching darkness

　　（B）we decided to ask for advice as the darkness

　　（C）and because the darkness was approching, we decided to ask for advice

　　（D）we decided to ask for advice because the darkness was approching

　　＜解答＞　C（主要子句）

692. I firmly believe that for this purpose, _____.

　　（A）light, glossy and durable paper only should be used

　　（B）everybody except me would like to use light glossy, and durable paper

　　（C）light, glossy paper that stands hard wear should be used

　　（D）only light, glossy and durable paper should be used

　　＜解答＞　D（字序）

693. After considering all necessary factors, the author was of that the next cost of the goods produced should be_____.

　　（A）about time

　　（B）highest

　　（C）much more higher

　　（D）somewhat higher

　　＜解答＞　D（形容詞）

694. His class began at 9:00 and he was_____.

　　（A）at time

　　（B）on time

　　（C）timely

（D）in time

<解答> B（修飾片語）

695. The government warned people_____crannyberries because they were contaminated with insecticides.

（A）not to eat

（B）to not eat

（C）in not eating

（D）to eat not

<解答> A（否定的不定詞）

696. The way of our thinking is influenced_____.

（A）at large by cultural factors

（B）largely by cultural factors

（C）by cultural factors at large

（D）by cultural factors largely

<解答> B（字序）

697. He told me_____.

（A）that I have just told them

（B）the same as I have just told them

（C）what I have just told them

（D）as that I have told them

<解答> C（名詞附屬子句）

698. The jeweler told them that_____.

（A）diamonds were a good investment

（B）diamonds were a good investing

（C）investing in diamonds were good

（D）investment with diamonds was good

<解答> A（名詞附屬子句）

699. The building looked beautiful, but_____.

（A）inferior it was in construction

（B）it was constructed poorly

(C) it was having inferior construction

(D) the constructing of it was terrible

<解答> B（副詞附屬子句）

700. _____ by the decision, the lawyer left the courtroom qucikly.

(A) Being angry

(B) Angered

(C) For angering

(D) To anger

<解答> B（縮減的副詞子句）

701. We could not understand the lecture because_____.

(A) the microphone did not work well

(B) working not well was the microphone

(C) not working well was the microphone

(D) the microphone was working not well

<解答> A（副詞附屬子句）

702. He can remember the past more accurately and more vividly than_____.

(A) neither of his parents remember

(B) either his parents are able to

(C) his parents can

(D) memory of his parents have

<解答> C（比較）

703. The reinforcement of our national defense is the best way to prevent_____.

(A) us to be attacked by enemy

(B) our enemy to attack us

(C) us from being attacked

(D) the enemy against attacking

<解答> C（代名詞的一致性）

704. _____, his mother had not approved of his study program.

(A) Since he left for school

(B) After he left for school

（C）Because he left for school

（D）When he left for school

　　＜解答＞ A（副詞附屬子句）

705. Janice was pleased to learn＿＿＿.

（A）how well her son is being handled

（B）her son got improved

（C）how well her son had handled himself

（D）how improvement achieved her son

　　＜解答＞ C（名詞附屬子句）

706. She died when she was ninety, not of old age, but＿＿＿ when she fell down from a flight of stairs.

（A）that she injured her head

（B）of when her head was injured

（C）because she injured her head

（D）for injuring her head

　　＜解答＞ D（修飾的片語）

707. People who work hard＿＿＿.

（A）are not necessarily rewarded by a successful result

（B）are not necessarily a success result

（C）do not necessarily receive the successful result

（D）do not necessarily succeed

　　＜解答＞ D（避免冗長）

708. The principal responsibility of managing the dormitory rests with the students＿＿＿.

（A）itself

（B）of itself

（C）themselves

（D）theirselves

　　＜解答＞ C（代名詞的一致性）

709. My brother seldom does his homework in the morning.＿＿＿.

（A）So does John

（B）John is too

（C）John doesn't too

（D）Nor does John

＜解答＞　D（縮減的副詞子句）

710.　Mary keeps talking about the party- she had a very good time, _____she?

（A）hadn't

（B）had

（C）didn't

（D）weren't

＜解答＞　C（附加問題）

711.　It is necessary that an efficient worker_____ his work on time.

（A）accomplishes

（B）can accomplish

（C）accomplish

（D）has accomplished

＜解答＞　C（假設語氣）

712.　I didn't go to the party, but I do wish I_____ there.

（A）was

（B）were

（C）had been

（D）went

＜解答＞　C（假設語氣）

713.　I didn't ask him to do such a hard job. In fact, I don't expect him_____
impossibilities.

（A）did

（B）do

（C）to do

（D）does

＜解答＞　C（不定詞）

714. Tom isn't the tallest boy in the class, but he is taller than＿＿ students.

   （A）any of the

   （B）some

   （C）any other

   （D）some of the

   ＜解答＞ D（比較）

715. Helen does't know how much I spent in repairing the house; if she ever found out, I'm sure＿＿.

   （A）she'd never forgive me

   （B）she never forgives me

   （C）she'll never forgive me

   （D）she does never forgive me

   ＜解答＞ A（副詞附屬子句）

716. They don't seem to answer their phone whenever I call. There isn't anyone at home, ＿＿?

   （A）isn't there

   （B）is there

   （C）is it

   （D）isn't it

   ＜解答＞ B（附加問題）

717. My watch is broken. I must have it＿＿.

   （A）repairing

   （B）to be repaired

   （C）to be repairing

   （D）repaired

   ＜解答＞ D（過去分詞）

718. I bite my nails. I must break＿＿.

   （A）the habit to me

   （B）the habit with myself

   （C）myself of the habit

（D）of the habit myself

<解答>　C（字序）

719. I should have gone to the opera yesterday. It was very good. I wish I_____ yesterday off.

（A）have had

（B）had

（C）have

（D）had had

<解答>　D（假設語氣）

720. Mary's mother got sick, so she_____.

（A）called her party on

（B）called her party of

（C）called her party off

（D）called on her party

<解答>　C（副詞附屬子句）

721. She is studing medical science now but she_____ a lawyer.

（A）would be

（B）used to be

（C）formerly were

（D）had been

<解答>　B（副詞附屬子句）

722. I didn't know this Picasso exhibit was closed, but I wouldn't have been able to come even if_____ about it.

（A）knew

（B）I'd known

（C）I have been knowing

（D）I've known

<解答>　B（條件句）

723. I know this is the right train. The ticket agent said it would be on_____.

（A）Track Two

　（B）the Track Second

　（C）Second Track

　（D）the two Track

　＜解答＞　A（名詞+基數）

724. Just look at this room. My roommate_____ up his clothes.

　（A）is never hanging

　（B）does never hang

　（C）never hangs

　（D）never hanged

　＜解答＞　C（動詞時態）

725. How many brand-new cars there are! Automobile production in the last ten years has increased_____.

　（A）highly

　（B）infinitely

　（C）in the large scale

　（D）greatly

　＜解答＞　D（副詞）

726. Since they are moving to a new house, they have to buy_____ furniture.

　（A）many

　（B）quite a few

　（C）a lot of

　（D）a few

　＜解答＞　C（形容詞）

727. Nancy isn't here. It's my fault. I forgot all about_____ her.

　（A）telephoning

　（B）to telephone

　（C）to telephone to

　（D）the telephoning to

　＜解答＞　A（動詞）

728. I like eating in the cafeteria. I like_____ food.

（A）almost all the

（B）the most of

（C）nearly all of

（D）almost of the

＜解答＞　A（副詞和形容詞的位置）

729.　He is not supposed to play with us until the manager recommends that

he_____ a member of this club.

（A）be

（B）is

（C）they

（D）that

＜解答＞　A（假設語氣）

730.　Would you like to see the movie tonight? I_____ meet you at the gate of the

Students Center.

（A）　would

（B）　will

（C）　must

（D）　ought to

＜解答＞　B（助動詞）

731.　John is very diligent. But his pay is not_____ for his work.

（A）enough good

（B）good enough

（C）as good enough

（D）good as enough

＜解答＞　B（字序）

732.　I must go there earlier. John has suggested that I_____ an hour before the

discussion begins.

（A）go

（B）shall go

（C）will go

（D）would go

　　＜解答＞　A（假設語氣）

733.　I cannot come to your dinner party tonight. I really would be＿＿＿.

　　（A）glad

　　（B）glad to have

　　（C）glad to

　　（D）glad to do it

　　＜解答＞　C（縮減的副詞子句）

734.　They say it was disastrous fire. It had Jone out of＿＿＿ for a while.

　　（A）head

　　（B）sight

　　（C）hand

　　（D）place

　　＜解答＞　C（介詞片語）

735.　Weather＿＿＿, the picnic will be held as scheduled.

　　（A）ermits

　　（B）should permit

　　（C）will permit

　　（D）permitting

　　＜解答＞　D（縮減的副詞子句）

736.　Because his parents disapproved of a major in physical education, William reluctantly decided on civil engineering＿＿＿.

　　（A）for a second alternative

　　（B）to make another choice

　　（C）as a second choice

　　（D）for another alternative

　　＜解答＞　C（修飾的片語）

737.　Until recently, land in large areas of Slockholm belonged either to the crown or to the city; there was＿＿＿ thing as private ownership of land.

　　（A）not such a

（B）no such

（C）not such

（D）not any

＜解答＞ B（形容詞）

738. The judge asked me many questions and_____.

（A）they had difficulty being answered

（B）answering them was with difficulty

（C）they were difficult to answer

（D）to answer them was to be difficult

＜解答＞ C（對等連接詞）

739. I came to lunch so early because I thought the bell had already_____.

（A）rang

（B）ring

（C）been rang

（D）rung

＜解答＞ D（過去分詞）

740. The streets are all wet. It_____ during the night.

（A）must be raining

（B）must have been rain

（C）had to rain

（D）must have rained

＜解答＞ D（動詞時態）

741. The policeman let those boys go, hoping they would learn from their mistake_____ the rules in the future.

（A）and to obey

（B）and be obedient to

（C）and obey

（D）to be obedient to

＜解答＞ C（對等連接詞）

742. Jennnifer hates to do her homework. In fact, no one_____ it.

（A）ever really enjoys doing

（B）really is ever enjoying to do

（C）enjoys to really ever do

（D）really ever enjoys to do

＜解答＞ A（字序）

743. As to those individuals who try to avoid paying their share of the costs of governments, _____.

（A）should be given special attention to the fact in view

（B）they should be vigorously prosecuted

（C）and the supports of the people should, more or less, extending

（D）we hereby bid our goodbye to you

＜解答＞ B（主要子句）

744. I think that_____.

（A）his coat is different from that one

（B）the information be correct

（C）Mary is as beautiful like that girl

（D）I don't remember how did Joe get it

＜解答＞ A（名詞附屬子句）

745. It is said that_____.

（A）the doctor operated in him yesterday

（B）the new film is Aloving story

（C）he has received many mails

（D）she always has her nails manicured

＜解答＞ D（名詞附屬子句）

746. Imagine our embarrassment when we girls saw Martha_____.

（A）sat with her beau in the front row

（B）she is sitting with her beau in the front row

（C）sitting with her beau in the front row

（D）to sit with her beau in the front row

＜解答＞ C（現在分詞）

747. Do you believe that_____?
     （A）the meeting of the committee held in the Rose room
     （B）he will study the lesson providing he could find his book
     （C）he decided to open a book store
     （D）if he lays down on the job, he will regret it
     ＜解答＞ C（名詞附屬子句）

748. He is interesting himself actively_____.
     （A）of participating in that business
     （B）as that of his
     （C）in the affair
     （D）on continuing his education
     ＜解答＞ C（修飾的片語）

749. To support the idea that some inflation is not necessarily an economic evil is known_____.
     （A）by Afamous musician
     （B）by an economist
     （C）by Aperson of his speciality
     （D）by whom he knows
     ＜解答＞ B（修飾的片語）

750. By Supreme Court decisions, the principle has been established that a state can be prevented from infringing upon freedom of speech and the press _____.
     （A）only if its constitution provides a guarantee for such infringement
     （B）because freedom of speech and the press are considered being basic liberties protected on the Fourteenth Amendment against state action
     （C）because the first ten amendments are limitations upon either the
     （D）under the " due process " clause of the Fifth Amendment
     ＜解答＞ A（副詞附屬子句）

751. Jefferson's Administration demonstrated its disagreement with the Hamiltonian System by_____.

（A）sharp reducting the tariff on imports

（B）abolish the excise tax

（C）repealing the Alien and Sedition laws

（D）to abolish the bank on the United States

＜解答＞ C（現在分詞）

752. The dead professor had been_____.

（A）a gifted amateur musician, an outstanding physicist, and a Nobel Prize winner

（B）brave and an associate professor

（C）an outstanding physicist, a gifted amateur musician, and a Nobel Prize winner

（D）a Nobel Prize winner, an outstanding physicist, and a gifted amateur musician

＜解答＞ A（平行構句）

753. I am sure glad to_____.

（A）happily receive you

（B）doing that for you

（C）received you happily

（D）receive you at the party

＜解答＞ D（不定詞）

754. Her wages as a truck-driver were considerably higher_____.

（A）in comparison to the wages of a ditch-digger

（B）than aditch-digger

（C）if not higher than, better than a ditch-digger

（D）than that of a ditch-digger

＜解答＞ D（比較）

755. Speeders_____.

（A）either have to go to a school where they study traffic problems or to jail

（B）have either to go to a school where they study traffic problem or to jail

（C）has to go either to a school where they study traffic problems or to jail

（D）have to go either to a school where they study traffic problems or to jail

＜解答＞ D（動詞+字序）

756. He believes that_____.

（A）as he rose to an altitude of 10,000 feet, the distant mountains to raise with us

（B）scarcity to food caused prices to raise

（C）the wounded man raised himself up and called for help

（D）the monument was still sitting where the pioneers had set it

＜解答＞ D（名詞附屬子句）

757. New York State is larger than_____.

（A）any other northeastern state

（B）any of the notheastern states

（C）any the northeastern states

（D）other northeastern states

＜解答＞ A（比較）

758. The Sunday evenings continued through all the changes_____.

（A）in its turns

（B）in his turns

（C）in our lives

（D）in our life

＜解答＞ C（修飾的片語）

759. To dance gracefully and confidently, _____.

（A）practice is important to you

（B）one needs a certain amount of practice

（C）they must be practice it

（D）a certain amount of practice is needed

＜解答＞ B（主詞）

760. Mr. Cleary will take the party of girls to the station and make sure that_____.

（A）all of them will have their tickets

（B）she will have her tickets

（C）you all will have your tickets

（D）all of them will have his tickets

＜解答＞　A（名詞附屬子句）

761.　In all of the workers, union_____.

（A）they having definite and detailed rules about pension

（B）there are definite and detailed rules about pension

（C）they have definite and detailed rules about pension

（D）they had definite and detailed rules about pension

＜解答＞　B（主詞）

762.　Upon hearing the bell, _____.

（A）the students' departure was hasty

（B）out departure was hasty

（C）we departed hastily

（D）the classroom was filled immediately

＜解答＞　C（主詞）

763.　I have to justify a man's refusal to fight for his country on the grounds that_____.

（A）you should contribute what we have to do for our country

（B）you should not be forced to violate your conscientious scruples

（C）he should not be forced to violate his conscientious scruples

（D）they should not be forced to violate his conscientious scruples

＜解答＞　C（副詞附屬子句）

764.　First be sure that you have brought your baggage, and then_____.

（A）you should be certain if you have brought with you enough money

（B）the necessary medical supplies must be brought along with you

（C）you must not forget to phone your parents that you're going soon

（D）remember that you should bring some money with you

＜解答＞　D（對等連接詞）

765.　Frank knew that he was potentially an alcoholic again and_____.

（A）that no alcohol at all should pass his lips

（B）drink no more

（C）he should drink no more

（D）that he should pass no alcohol through his lips at all

＜解答＞ D（對等連接詞）

766. The majority of the consumers of today believe in the economic

system_____.

（A）in the time Twentieth Century has

（B）through which they can be benefited

（C）of the contemporary time of today

（D）under which the modern man of today lives

＜解答＞ D（修飾的片語）

767. We left the valley floor at eight in the morning_____.

（A）and the rim of canyon was reached by noon

（B）and arrived the rim of canyon by noon

（C）and the rim of canyon was met by boon

（D）and reached the rim of canyon by noon

＜解答＞ D（對等連接詞）

768. The day I was supposed to leave, _____.

（A）I realize I still haven't received my passport and visa

（B）I had no idea how much was there going to do

（C）I had no idea how much there is to do and I waited too long before I

began getting ready

（D）I simply couldn't believe the time had passed so fast

＜解答＞ D（主要子句）

769. I certainly think that_____.

（A）my aunt didn't hire an apartment

（B）to lease a typist seems necessary

（C）the deperately sick man had an illusion of great strength and power

（D）as a citizen of the United States, I should demand to know why am I

being held by foreign authorities

<解答> C（名詞附屬子句）

770. The double-breasted suit does not look well on Ernest, _____.

（A）he never does look his best in them

（B）never does it look his best in his suit

（C）he never does look his best in it

（D）his suit never does look his best on him

<解答> C（字序）

771. We had just started the third rubber of bridge when, looking up, _____.

（A）there was the host

（B）the host was there

（C）we found the host

（D）we see the host

<解答> C（副詞附屬子句）

772. Although he was warned, _____.

（A）but he persisted in his evil ways

（B）I have not found him completely happy

（C）he acted as alternative to the delegate elected

（D）he allowed his students a good deal of freedom

<解答> D（主要子句）

773. Take exercise_____.

（A）whenever you will have time

（B）or otherwise you will be missing it

（C）while you shall have to work

（D）if you want to keep well before breakfast

<解答> D（副詞附屬子句）

774. We are not able to forecast the possible fluctuations of climate condition_____.

（A）that lay before us

（B）that rise before us

（C）that sit before us

（D）that lie before us

＜解答＞　D（形容詞附屬子句）

775. But whatever the truth of the matter, _____.

（A）I wish to go to bed

（B）I was very surprised

（C）I do to accomplish my duty

（D）I am to admire that first part of " Howl "

＜解答＞　D（主詞和動詞的位置）

776. Tom Simson not only put all his worldly store at the disposal of Mr.

Oakhurst, _____.

（A）but wishes to be alone

（B）but he became a hermit

（C）but he wasn't happy at all

（D）but seemed to enjoy the prospect of their enforced seclusion

＜解答＞　D（連接詞一致性）

777. But far more meaningful to us than imitation_____.

（A）are discipline and self-criticism

（B）is self-criticism and discipline

（C）comes self-criticism and discipline

（D）we should emphasize discipline and self-criticism

＜解答＞　A（倒裝句）

778. Such apparently effortless writing is actually the result of long practice

and_____.

（A）study much

（B）studied much

（C）much to be studied

（D）much study

＜解答＞　D（字序）

779. The typewriter_____.

（A）was lying on the table, where it had been laid all week

（B）was laying on the table, where it had been laid all week

（C）was laying on the table, where it had laid all week

（D）was lying on the table, where it had laid all week

＜解答＞　A（動詞時態）

780.　The wind lulls as if_____.

（A）they feared to wake it

（B）it feared to waken them

（C）it fears to decrease them

（D）it is going to awaken them

＜解答＞　B（假設語氣）

781.　We turn to books in moments of_____.

（A）sorrow, having boredom, or solitude is with us

（B）sorrow, boredom, or solitude

（C）sorrow and solitude as well of boredom

（D）sorrow that attacks us

＜解答＞　B（平行構句）

782.　He made the mistake of joining two clubs which took a great deal of time_____.

（A）which he could have been studying in

（B）from which he might have studied

（C）which was studying time to him

（D）that he could have used for study

＜解答＞　D（形容詞附屬子句）

783.　When he was asked why his friend had not accepted the offer, he_____.

（A）suggested that his friend's pride prevented him from accepting

（B）hinted pride being the reason his friend didn't accept

（C）stated as the reason for his friends not accepting as pride

（D）implied his friend's nonacceptance was resulting from pride

＜解答＞　A（主要子句）

784. Though his paintings showed a high degree of technical skill, they were not the kind_____.

　　（A）to have a very wide appeal

　　（B）to attract the bulk of the people

　　（C）to interest people on a broad basis

　　（D）to make the masses fond of them

　　＜解答＞　A（修飾的片語）

785. He was cold_____.

　　（A）most of the night

　　（B）much through the night

　　（C）many parts of the night

　　（D）much of the night

　　＜解答＞　A（副詞片語）

786. John never realize that, in order to play the piano, he must have_____.

　　（A）not only training but talent also

　　（B）also training and talent

　　（C）not talent but training also

　　（D）only training but also talent

　　＜解答＞　A（連接詞形式）

787. To the very complicated situation the officers_____.

　　（A）had to pay much attention to it

　　（B）have some of their attention to be paid

　　（C）had to pay more of their attention

　　（D）paid no attention to

　　＜解答＞　C（動詞+不定詞）

788. Compared to those of a hundred years ago, the airplanes are technically more complex, and_____.

　　（A）its speed greatly increases

　　（B）their speed are greatly increased

　　（C）they are faster than ever before

（D）the modern planes are faster

＜解答＞ C（對等連接詞）

789. There comes a time in every man's life_____.

（A）then he has to think

（B）which he needs

（C）when he has to think

（D）therefore he has to work hard

＜解答＞ C（副詞附屬子句）

790. Indeed, it is a grim world, _____.

（A）and the future looks dark

（B）but the future is dark

（C）man must work hard

（D）and there are scientific discoveries

＜解答＞ A（對等連接詞）

791. Hadrdly had he mailed the letter_____.

（A）than he began to regret writing it

（B）when he began to regret writing it

（C）when he mailed it

（D）then he received one

＜解答＞ A（連接詞＋倒裝句）

792. According to this account, he was a tender, home-loving father, _____.

（A）who likes to play with his children

（B）whom loved to tell his children stories

（C）who liked to be with his children

（D）who enjoys being with his children

＜解答＞ C（形容詞附屬子句）

793. Many guests for the party who did not receive this information would not

show up_____.

（A）but wouldn't come anyway

（B）and no notice could be given in time

（C）and would possible come

（D）to join us

＜解答＞ D（修飾的片語）

794.　Tom's schoolmates at the college still talk about him as an excellent writer＿＿＿.

（A）and he taught at the college, too

（B）good football player

（C）who also played football

（D）and a good football player

＜解答＞ D（連接詞一致性）

795.　I had supposed that no one would ever produce a book on this subject to which I agree; ＿＿＿.

（A）but Professor Baker has now done the impossible

（B）yet even their clever style cannot conceal their lack of real understanding

（C）but his most recent book is one in which the above description can quite justly applied

（D）and the latest book of his will, also, contribute every few

＜解答＞ A（副詞附屬子句）

796.　Although Asimoy still holds the title of associate professor of biochemistry at Boston University Medical School, ＿＿＿.

（A）his teaching duties are now confined to occasional lectures

（B）he doesn't permit to give lectures freely

（C）the teaching duties of him are normally limited to usual lectures

（D）lectures are only occasonally given as teaching duties

＜解答＞ A（主要子句）

797.　When the meeting was beginning, the president reported the program and advised＿＿＿.

（A）the students first reading it quickly and outlined it

（B）first the students quickly reading it and outlined it

（C）first reading it quickly and outlined it

（D）first quickly reading it and outlined it

＜解答＞ C（字序）

798. I doubt_____.

（A）whether he can come

（B）if he can come or not

（C）while he will be here

（D）what will he do

＜解答＞ A（名詞附屬子句）

799. Before writing a book, _____.

（A）the first thing is to consider what to say

（B）you must first ponder what to say and what not to be said carefully

（C）it's extemely necessary that you know what to say

（D）you must first ponder what to say and what not to say carefully

＜解答＞ D（主詞）

800. Everybody knows that_____.

（A）he neither has nor can sell this coat at so low a figure

（B）he neither has nor he sell this coat at such a low figure

（C）he neither has sold or can sell this coat at such a low figure

（D）he neither has sold nor can sell this coat at such a low price

＜解答＞ D（名詞附屬子句）

801. There will always remain some citizens_____.

（A）which will support it

（B）whoever will accept the idea

（C）who just don't care enough to exercise their franchise

（D）that ideas he accepted

＜解答＞ C（形容詞附屬子句）

802. What type of automobile would you buy_____?

（A）if you have free choice to choose the cars available today

（B）if you are free to choose among all the cars available today

（C）if all the cars available were free to be chosen by you

（D）if you were free to choose among all the cars available today

＜解答＞ D（假設語氣）

803. Sometimes we feel such disappointments_____.

（A）so strong that we can no longer work as sleep

（B）so strongly that we can't no longer work as sleep

（C）so strongly that working and sleeping are no longer with us

（D）so strongly that we can no longer work and sleep

＜解答＞ D（副詞附屬子句）

804. The theory of public opinion is usually regarded by the public as_____.

（A）controversial

（B）enough reasonable

（C）practical significant

（D）principally importance

＜解答＞ A（形容詞）

805. "As for your going along with us, " she said, " _____"

（A）my husband and myself certainly have no objection

（B）certainly my husband and I have no objection

（C）either I or my husband certainly have no objection

（D）either my husband or I certainly have no objection

＜解答＞ D（主詞）

806. The sun_____ early in the summer.

（A）rise up

（B）roses

（C）rises

（D）rises up

＜解答＞ C（動詞）

807. The day was so_____ that we decided to take a picnic lunch to the beach.

（A）clear and warmly

（B）clearly and warmly

(C) clearly and warm

(D) clear and warm

<解答> D（形容詞）

808. Would you like to go_____ a ride?

(A) with

(B) on

(C) for

(D) in

<解答> C（介詞）

809. There was_____ of complete silence.

(A) an instant

(B) hours

(C) three minutes

(D) second

<解答> A（名詞）

810. Let's go find out_____.

(A) home she is whether or not

(B) whether at home

(C) whether home she is or not

(D) whether or not she is home

<解答> D（連接詞+字序）

811. _____ on television can be very damaging to children who watch the programs.

(A) The too great sex and violence

(B) Sex and violence too much

(C) The great numbers of sex and violence

(D) Too much sex and violence

<解答> D（主詞+形容詞）

812. _____ of the children is sick today.

(A) One

(B) Fewer

(C) Many

(D) Some

<解答> A（主詞和動詞的一致性）

813. The man＿＿＿ is my brother-in-law.

(A) of the dark beard

(B) with the dark beard

(C) to the dark beard

(D) with the dark beard on

<解答> B（修飾的片語）

814. They were here, but they've gone to＿＿＿ apartment.

(A) they'rs

(B) theirs

(C) his

(D) their

<解答> D（代名詞形式）

815. It was so＿＿＿ done that John felt like applauding.

(A) beautiful

(B) beautifully

(C) good

(D) fine

<解答> B（副詞）

816. I've had＿＿＿ time to decide.

(A) than enough more

(B) more than enough

(C) than more enough

(D) enough than more

<解答> B（字序）

817. Alex could not start his car because＿＿＿.

(A) of not knowing where to find his key

（B）where his key was he didn't know

（C）he didn't know where his key was

（D）to find his key he did not know where

＜解答＞　C（副詞附屬子句）

818.　Henry decided＿＿＿ his new suit.

（A）to have worn

（B）to wore

（C）to wear

（D）to weared

＜解答＞　C（不定詞）

819.　When Anita got to class, she was horrified＿＿＿ to study for the test.

（A）discovering she forgot

（B）at discovering she had forgotten

（C）to discover she had forgotten

（D）to discover she forgot

＜解答＞　C（不定詞）

820.　＿＿＿ us are staying home.

（A）Some

（B）A little

（C）Couple

（D）Less

＜解答＞　A（主詞）

821.　＿＿＿ if we walk on the grass?

（A）Do you want

（B）Do they mind

（C）Are we minded

（D）Can you allow

＜解答＞　B（主要子句）

822.　I think she＿＿＿ right now.

（A）studying

（B）is studied

（C）is studying

（D）to study

<解答> C（名詞附屬子句）

823. Jack would have gone to Chicago_____ to get a plane reservation.

（A）was he able

（B）would he be able

（C）if he is able

（D）if he had been able

<解答> D（條件句）

824. Everyone is responsible for_____ own composition.

（A）his

（B）their

（C）nobody's

（D）all their

<解答> A（代名詞一致性）

825. Reaching the top of the mountain, we_____ energy left for the descent.

（A）had hardly any

（B）hadn't hardly any

（C）had hardly no

（D）hadn't hardly no

<解答> A（動詞+避免雙重否定）

826. There isn't_____ food in the house.

（A）none

（B）no

（C）some

（D）any

<解答> D（形容詞）

827. It's Robert's job_____ the dogs and put out the cat.

（A）food

（B）having fed

（C）to feed

（D）has fed

＜解答＞ C（不定詞）

828. May I read over_____ for the classes I missed?

（A）lecture notes yours

（B）you lecture notes

（C）lecture notes of your

（D）your lecture notes

＜解答＞ D（字序）

829. _____ of all of the 1980 presidential candidates was Ronald Reagan.

（A）The richest

（B）The richer

（C）The most richly

（D）The rich

＜解答＞ A（比較）

830. Tomorrow at 8:00 Laura has to_____ history examination.

（A）pass

（B）take

（C）succeed

（D）fail

＜解答＞ B（不定詞）

831. The play_____ the typical a merican tourist.

（A）poked fun at

（B）made the audience to laugh at

（C）made Amockery to

（D）joked at

＜解答＞ A（動詞）

832. I could have done better if I_____ more time.

（A）have had

（B）had

（C）had had

（D）will have had

＜解答＞ C（條件句）

833. They_____ so that we wouldn't recognize them.

（A）costumed

（B）disguised

（C）were disguising

（D）were disguised

＜解答＞ D（被動語態）

834. I will talk to the children_____.

（A）one and then the other

（B）first one thenthe next

（C）one by one

（D）in single

＜解答＞ C（修飾的片語）

835. Misfortunes like that aren't_____ fault.

（A）each

（B）anybody

（C）no one's

（D）anybody's

＜解答＞ D（所有格）

836. They're not very good, but I like_____.

（A）anyway to play ball with them

（B）to play ball with them anyway

（C）to play with them ball anyway

（D）with them anyway to play ball

＜解答＞ B（不定詞+字序）

837. _____ political parties in this election----Democrats, Republicans, and Independents.

（A）There are three

（B）There being three

（C）The three

（D）Three

<解答> A（形式上的或虛假的主詞+動詞）

838. I asked her_____ was on the phone.

（A）which

（B）who

（C）whom

（D）whomever

<解答> B（名詞附屬子句）

839. He doesn't know_____ about sports.

（A）nothing

（B）anything

（C）at all

（D）something

<解答> B（名詞）

840. While he_____ the poster, a door somewhere behind him opened.

（A）is staring at

（B）did stare to

（C）looked carefully upon

（D）was staring at

<解答> D（副詞附屬子句）

841. Richard's expression_____ cat enjoying a saucer of milk.

（A）looking like a

（B）looked as a

（C）like

（D）was like that of a

<解答> D（動詞）

842. That was the year_____ I was born.

(A) where

(B) into which

(C) in which

(D) at which

<解答> C（形容詞附屬子句）

843. After_____ on his couch more than a dozen times, he gave up his attempt to sleep.

(A) he overturned

(B) turning over

(C) his having over

(D) turning up

<解答> B（縮減的副詞子句）

844. Nancy has classes on Monday, Wednesday, and Friday, three days_____.

(A) until a week

(B) during a week

(C) a week

(D) for a week

<解答> C（副詞片語）

845. ____, Solomon smoked with moody composure.

(A) From an out view

(B) Outwardly

(C) On the outside

(D) Out

<解答> B（副詞）

846. _____ in this city will you find any store open on Sundays.

(A) There is scarcely any place

(B) In hardly places

(C) Hardly any place

(D) No place barely any place

<解答> C（倒裝句）

847. He_____ move the piano in.

（A）helped in to

（B）does help for us

（C）helped ourselves

（D）helped us

＜解答＞ D（動詞）

848. Carol refused; _____, her answer was " no."

（A）in other words

（B）otherwise

（C）words for words

（D）however

＜解答＞ A（副詞片語）

849. Desperation is a lamentable_____ courage.

（A）standby for

（B）substitute for

（C）replacement with

（D）turning for

＜解答＞ B（名詞+介詞）

850. When Carl met his wife at the airport, he_____.

（A）a kiss game her in the cheek

（B）gave her a kiss on the cheek

（C）gave a kiss to her cheek

（D）by the cheek gave her a kiss

＜解答＞ B（字序）

851. The stolen jawls must be recovered, _____.

（A）at any cost

（B）to any cost

（C）with any expense

（D）no matter any expenditure

＜解答＞ A（修飾的片語）

852. The assassination attempt_____ millions, because the speech was on television.

    （A）was seen by

    （B）was saw by

    （C）seen by

    （D）was seen for

    ＜解答＞ A（被動語態）

853. Don't let me disturb you; please get_____ your typing.

    （A）with

    （B）in with

    （C）on with

    （D）in

    ＜解答＞ C（動詞片語+介詞）

854. At his death the elder Boardman_____ certain heirlooms and a small sum in cash.

    （A）deposited

    （B）left after him

    （C）left behind

    （D）left ahead

    ＜解答＞ C（動詞+副詞）

855. Those were the soldiers_____ to save the town.

    （A）whose responsibility it was

    （B）in whom there was a responsibility

    （C）whose was the responsibility

    （D）from whom the responsibility came

    ＜解答＞ A（形容詞附屬子句）

856. _____ ten people waiting for the bus.

    （A）There is

    （B）There wasn't

    （C）There was

（D）There were

＜解答＞ D（虛假的主詞+動詞）

857. As I_____ I suddenly remembered that it was your birthday.

（A）to feed my cats

（B）am feeding my cats

（C）had fed my cats

（D）was feeding my cats

＜解答＞ D（副詞附屬子句）

858. Real wealth is_____ avoid doing what one would rather not.

（A）being able as to

（B）to be able to

（C）to

（D）to find yourself able to

＜解答＞ B（不定詞片語）

859. This test is for students_____ native language is not English.

（A）that

（B）whose

（C）of whom

（D）which

＜解答＞ B（形容詞附屬子句）

860. He had a strong_____ regard the gardener as a thief.

（A）reluctance to

（B）feeling of reluctance to

（C）attitude not to

（D）negation to

＜解答＞ A（名詞）

861. If you need an extra bed for your guest, you can use one_____.

（A）our

（B）us

（C）of ours

（D）of us

＜解答＞ C（代名詞形式）

862. Marilyn doesn't have_____ gas in her car.

（A）some

（B）no

（C）lots

（D）any

＜解答＞ D（形容詞）

863. Before anyone could do anything, the boat slowly_____.

（A）sinks

（B）was sinking

（C）sank

（D）was sank

＜解答＞ C（動詞時態）

864. If he_____ the storekeeper's scissors, he would have forgotten to buy a pair.

（A）would of seen

（B）had not seen

（C）had not of seen

（D）has seen

＜解答＞ B（條件句）

865. They_____ a meeting for Saturday night.

（A）hoped

（B）having arranged

（C）deciding

（D）planned

＜解答＞ D（動詞）

866. After he failed the exam, his mood_____ despair.

（A）verged into

（B）became close to

（C）bordered on

（D）inclined upon

<解答> C（主要子句）

867. Billy Carter hurt his brother's chances_____.

（A）on a reelection

（B）into getting elected again

（C）for reelection

（D）reelecting

<解答> C（修飾的片語）

868. I have been trying to contact her_____ the past week.

（A）since

（B）for

（C）through

（D）inside

<解答> B（介詞）

869. The cat jumped_____ my lap.

（A）beside

（B）away

（C）into

（D）by

<解答> C（介詞）

870. Isabel can't stand it_____ noises during a concert.

（A）when people do

（B）if the music is disturbed by people'

（C）if people have

（D）when people make

<解答> D（副詞附屬子句）

871. Little boys like_____ trees.

（A）climb

（B）climbing

（C）swing from

（D）having Aswing

＜解答＞ B（動名詞）

872. She＿＿＿ from a fall by catching the railing.

（A）prevented herself

（B）saved herself

（C）stopped

（D）held her own self

＜解答＞ B（動詞）

873. The price of gasoline, about 50¢ a gallon not too long ago, ＿＿＿.

（A）now is too expensive for many car owners

（B）is too much costly for so many drivers

（C）cannot be bought by owners of cars easily

（D）makes it hard for a driver to use in his car

＜解答＞ A（動詞）

874. ＿＿＿ Albert is late, let's begin without him.

（A）Since

（B）Nevertheless

（C）However

（D）Consequently

＜解答＞ A（連接詞）

875. Despite his broken leg, Alan can walk＿＿＿ get around.

（A）good enough to

（B）good to

（C）well enough to

（D）fine enough to

＜解答＞ C（副詞）

876. The chickadee＿＿＿ a melodious song.

（A）sangs

（B）songs

（C）sings

（D）singed

＜解答＞ C（動詞）

877. Before a concert, the musicians_____ their instruments.

（A）tune in

（B）tune up

（C）tune to

（D）tune at

＜解答＞ B（動詞片語）

878. The fast_____ we have inflation makes it hard for families to buy the food they need.

（A）of

（B）that

（C）about

（D）since

＜解答＞ B（形容詞附屬子句）

879. He is wondering_____ a doctor.

（A）whether or not to see

（B）weather to see or not

（C）weather or not to see

（D）whether or not seeing

＜解答＞ A（連接詞）

880. If I can get_____ with my exams, I'll take a long vacation.

（A）under

（B）beyond

（C）behind

（D）through

＜解答＞ D（動詞片語）

881. When we get our tickets, _____ be marked " first class. "

（A）it is to

（B）it will

（C）they were to

（D）they will

＜解答＞ D（主要子句）

882. Please lend me_____ dollar.

（A）a

（B）an

（C）any

（D）a one

＜解答＞ A（冠詞）

883. I'm_____ all this garbage on the stairs.

（A）fed up at

（B）burned up for

（C）mad as the devil on

（D）sick and tired of

＜解答＞ D（對等連接詞）

884. _____, teachers, and parents all came to the rally for smaller classes.

（A）They were students

（B）There were students

（C）That students

（D）Students

＜解答＞ D（平行構句）

885. The dog_____ with the baby.

（A）made friends

（B）made friendly

（C）befriended

（D）befriending

＜解答＞ A（動詞）

886. When Mr. Kim needs a car, he uses_____.

（A）his son's

（B）that car of his son

（C）the car of his son

（D）his son's own car

＜解答＞　A（簡化）

887.　The lady spoke_____ to the child.

（A）very soft

（B）softly

（C）soft

（D）softly

＜解答＞　D（易混淆的字家族）

888.　Betty was_____ tired after she left the disco dance.

（A）kind of

（B）rather

（C）weakly

（D）real

＜解答＞　B（副詞）

889.　People who do not file an income tax return_____.

（A）it may prosecute

（B）may be prosecuted

（C）prosecution may follow

（D）they may be prosecuted

＜解答＞　B（動詞）

890.　Before Ted went to bed, he_____ the cat.

（A）was putting out

（B）put out

（C）had putted out

（D）had been putting out

＜解答＞　B（動詞時態）

891.　_____ my good advice, Jim walked home in the rain.

（A）Away from

（B）Contrary to

（C）The reverse of

（D）Rejecting himself of

＜解答＞ B（修飾的片語）

892. Her plane＿＿＿ at the airport right now.

（A）arrived

（B）was arriving

（C）has arrived

（D）is arriving

＜解答＞ D（動詞時態）

893. By the time Juan gets home, his aunt＿＿＿ for Puerto Rico.

（A）will leave

（B）leave

（C）will have left

（D）left

＜解答＞ C（動詞時態）

894. The wife of Steve Garvey, the baseball star, ＿＿＿ about being alone too often.

（A）bitterly has complained

（B）is being bitterly complaining

（C）having complained bitterly

（D）has been complaining bitterly

＜解答＞ D（字序）

895. Josette looked everywhere＿＿＿ her lost book.

（A）at

（B）to

（C）towards

（D）for

＜解答＞ D（介詞）

896. I went to the movie＿＿＿ I wanted to see John Wayne.

（A）although

（B）before

（C）as soon as

（D）because

＜解答＞ D（連接詞）

897. Kennedy＿＿＿ won the nomination if he hadn't had that unfortunate experience.

（A）could have

（B）could of

（C）will have

（D）would of

＜解答＞ A（條件句）

898. Mrs. Chou, ＿＿＿ husband is a diplomat, gives cooking lessons.

（A）whom

（B）who

（C）whose

（D）who's

＜解答＞ C（形容詞附屬子句）

899. To qualify for the job＿＿＿.

（A）a high school diploma is needed

（B）it is required that one has a high school diploma

（C）one need a high school diploma

（D）a diploma from high school is necessary

＜解答＞ C（主詞）

900. The Olympic Games, ＿＿＿ was not much of an event.

（A）without United States participation

（B）the United States not participating

（C）not participated in by the United States

（D）the United States failing to participate

＜解答＞ A（修飾的片語）

901. Petter asked Mark＿＿＿.

(A) where are the hammer

(B) where was the hammer

(C) where the hammer was

(D) where is the hammer

<解答>　C（字序）

902.　Mr. Andrews has not yet given me the receipts, but when_____ I'll mail them to you.

(A) he does

(B) they do

(C) he is

(D) they are

<解答>　A（縮減的副詞子句）

903.　The teacher made_____ their rubbers.

(A) the students take off

(B) the students to take off

(C) taking off the students of

(D) the students to take off

<解答>　A（沒有 to 的不定詞）

904.　Drinking liquor_____ on one's health.

(A) can effect dangerously

(B) can seriously affect

(C) seriously can effect

(D) seriously can endanger

<解答>　B（動詞）

905.　_____ a dancer myself I have excellent posture.

(A) Having being

(B) Being

(C) Having be

(D) To be

<解答>　B（分詞構句）

906. A large_____ of older-model cars do not have proper smog-control devices.

（A）many

（B）lot

（C）amount

（D）number

＜解答＞ D（形容詞片語）

907. Joe's pants were torn_____ up the tree.

（A）while climbing

（B）in climbing

（C）while he was climbing

（D）upon climbing

＜解答＞ C（副詞附屬子句）

908. When the school bell sounded, the children were_____ to run out of the classroom.

（A）all of them ready

（B）already

（C）all ready

（D）ready about

＜解答＞ C（易混淆的字）

909. The two new students_____ during the coffee break.

（A）being acquainted

（B）acquainting themselves

（C）got acquainted

（D）made known to each other

＜解答＞ C（動詞）

910. If Watergate_____ Nixon would not have resigned from the presidency.

（A）had not occurred

（B）did not occur

（C）was not occurring

（D）would not occur

<解答> A（條件句）

911. We are glad to_____ when you needed our help.

    （A）help you

    （B）help you along

    （C）having helped you

    （D）have helped you

    <解答> D（不定詞的過去式）

912. We have't seen you_____.

    （A）in the past four years

    （B）since four years

    （C）last four years

    （D）four years ago

    <解答> A（修飾的片語）

913. I can't do a good job today because I have a_____ headache.

    （A）lousy

    （B）stinking

    （C）bitchy

    （D）pounding

    <解答> D（形容詞）

914. _____ five laps around the track, Kenny was too tired to attend his German class.

    （A）To run

    （B）After running

    （C）He ran

    （D）Running

    <解答> B（分詞構句）

915. I would have said " Hello " if I_____ your brother.

    （A）could see

    （B）had seen

    （C）will see

（D）will have seen

＜解答＞ B（條件句）

916. The oldest applicant got the job because_____.

（A）his qualifications showed up the best

（B）he was the best one of qualifications

（C）he was the best qualified

（D）his was the best as qualified

＜解答＞ C（副詞附屬子句）

917. I think my answer on the exam was_____.

（A）the possible best choice

（B）the better of all choices

（C）the best possible choice

（D）best beyond all the choices

＜.解答:＞ C（字序）

918. The water_____ through the dam and rushed down into the vally below.

（A）busted

（B）burst

（C）bursted

（D）had busted

＜解答＞ B（動詞時態）

919. _____ are sought by an elementary school.

（A）Mentally retarded teachers

（B）Teachers retarded for mental cases

（C）Mental retarded case teachers

（D）Teachers for the mentally retarded

＜解答＞ D（主詞）

920. Miguel carefully_____ the wine into Carmen's glass.

（A）poured

（B）spilled

（C）spilled out

（D）poured away

＜解答＞ A（動詞）

921. The problem was with the battery＿＿＿ a dead cell.

（A）whcih having

（B）which had

（C）having

（D）in being with

＜解答＞ B（形容詞附屬子句）

922. President Carter greeted Eric Heiden＿＿＿ five gold medals at the Winter Olympics.

（A）who was the winner of

（B）winning

（C）by winning

（D）as he was the winner of

＜解答＞ A（形容詞附屬子句）

923. Mrs. Adams was injured＿＿＿.

（A）while preparing dinner for her husband in a horrible manner

（B）while preparing her husband's dinner in a horrible manner

（C）in a horrible manner while preparing her husband's dinner

（D）in a manner that was horrible in preparing her husband's dinner

＜解答＞ C（字序）

924. This toaster is＿＿＿ as the one you bought at Macy's.

（A）just as good

（B）equally as good

（C）good as

（D）equal as good

＜解答＞ A（副詞）

925. ＿＿＿, Ruggiero Ricci was considered a great violinist.

（A）At the age of six

（B）At six years old

（C）When age six

（D）When he was six years aged

＜解答＞　A（副詞片語）

926. Where should I put my hat? May I put it on_____.

（A）the hall table

（B）the talbe of hall

（C）hall's table

（D）hall table

＜解答＞　A（冠詞）

927. James has just arrived, but I didn't know he_____ until yesterday.

（A）will come

（B）was coming

（C）had been coming

（D）comes

＜解答＞　B（動詞時態）

928. I enjoyed the concert last night, they played_____ beautiful music.

（A）such

（B）such a

（C）so

（D）so a

＜解答＞　A（形容詞）

929. I walked 8 miles today. I never guessed that I could walk_____ far.

（A）that

（B）this

（C）such

（D）as

＜解答＞　A（副詞）

930. When her arm hit the chair she_____ her coffee.

（A）spilled

（B）overtook

（C）expired

（D）snarled

＜解答＞ A（動詞）

931. Many people favor＿＿＿ more nuclear power plants.

（A）to build

（B）built

（C）build

（D）building

＜解答＞ D（動名詞）

932. The setters at Jamestown lived on wild berries and roots because they

had＿＿＿ to eat.

（A）nothing else

（B）anything else

（C）something other

（D）nothing other

＜解答＞ A（名詞）

933. Officials warned consumers＿＿＿ certain shipments of cranberries that had

been contaminated by insecticides.

（A）to not eat

（B）not eating

（C）not to eat

（D）do not eat

＜解答＞ C（否定的不定詞）

934. ＿＿＿ the result of his first experiment was inconclusive, Dr. Johnson

continued to search for the new subatomic particle.

（A）Unless

（B）Before

（C）Although

（D）Whether

＜解答＞ C（副詞附屬子句）

935. Even though African game preserves have saved many animals, there
    are_____ that will not be saved.

    (A) some other

    (B) all others

    (C) many more

    (D) much more

    <解答> C（形容詞+可數名詞）

936. He isn't teaching piano now because he was tired of it; he_____.

    (A) decided to give it up

    (B) determined on stopping

    (C) decided giving up

    (D) decided give it up

    <解答> A（動詞+不定詞）

937. You will be able to make it to the tennis court; you'll get there_____.

    (A) anyhow

    (B) in a way

    (C) somehow

    (D) by some way

    <解答> C（副詞）

938. You look so tired tonight. It is time you_____.

    (A) go to sleep

    (B) went to sleep

    (C) go to bed

    (D) went to bed

    <解答> D（副詞附屬子句）

939. The Bakers arrived last night. If they'd only let us know earlier, _____ at the
    station.

    (A) we'd meet them

    (B) we'll meet them

    (C) we'd have met them

(D) we've met them

<解答> C（條件句）

940. I am sorry I lost the race, but I really wasn't fast enough to catch＿＿＿ the other runners.

(A) up

(B) up with

(C) to

(D) with

<解答> B（動詞片語）

941. I have given up trying to convince him; there is no point＿＿＿ with him.

(A) by arguing

(B) for arguing

(C) with arguing

(D) in arguing

<解答> D（介詞）

942. ＿＿＿, Mr. Wells is scarcely in sympathy with the working class.

(A) Being a socialist

(B) Since he is a socialist

(C) Although he is a socialist

(D) Despite he is a socialist

<解答> C（副詞附屬子句）

943. The student was delighted to be offered a summer job＿＿＿.

(A) that rewarded two dollars hourly

(B) that paid two dollars an hour

(C) with two-dollar pay in an hour

(D) with a pay of two-dollar per hour

<解答> B（形容詞附屬子句）

944. All＿＿＿ is a continuous supply of fuel oil.

(A) what is needed

(B) that is needed

（C）the thing needed

（D）for their needs

＜解答＞ B（形容詞附屬子句）

945. The violin will have to be carefully tuned before it_____.

（A）can be played

（B）is being played

（C）should play

（D）has to play

＜解答＞ A（副詞附屬子句）

946. _____ only after she understood microphsics that Dr. Weeks could complete her erperiments in molecular biology.

（A）It was

（B）It is

（C）There were

（D）There are

＜解答＞ A（it.....that 的構句）

947. Many wealthy families built their houses on the sites_____.

（A）on earlier Roman Villas

（B）of earlier Roman Villas

（C）in whcih Roman Villas have been

（D）when Roman Villas formerly domiciled

＜解答＞ B（修飾的片語）

948. Because of the revolt, the General assumed_____ as dictatorial role.

（A）it was described then

（B）that was described at that time

（C）what was described at the time

（D）what could be described for the time

＜解答＞ C（名詞附屬子句）

949. Tanbark was spread on the streets to_____ of traffic when Mr. Campbell was appearing on stage.

（A）leassen the sound

（B）deaden the noise

（C）decrease the voices

（D）take away the noise

＜解答＞ B（不定詞）

950. I have not found my book yet; in fact, I am not sure_____ I could have done with it.

（A）whether

（B）where

（C）when

（D）what

＜解答＞ D（名詞附屬子句）

951. I want to go to the dentist, but you_____ with me.

（A）need not to go

（B）do not need go

（C）need not go

（D）need go not

＜解答＞ C（副詞附屬子句）

952. Mr. Bundy is so strange today. And your manners_____ too.

（A）like this is

（B）are like his

（C）like he is

（D）like him are

＜解答＞ B（動詞）

953. Don't you know all of them are efficient_____?

（A）language teachers

（B）teaching language

（C）language teacher

（D）languages's teachers

＜解答＞ A（名詞當形容詞用）

954. Creater efforts to increase wheat production must be made if bread
shortages_____ avoided.
(A) will be
(B) can be
(C) are to be
(D) were to be
＜解答＞ C（動詞一致性）

955. The population of many Alaskan cities has_____doubled the past three years.
(A) larger than
(B) more than
(C) as great as
(D) as many as
＜解答＞ B（比較）

956. Martin has wanted to be a doctor since_____.
(A) he had ten years
(B) ten year old
(C) ten years of age
(D) he was ten
＜解答＞ D（副詞附屬子句）

957. If negotiations for the new trade agreements take_____, critical food
shortages will develop in several countries.
(A) too much longer
(B) much too long
(C) the longest
(D) the longer
＜解答＞ B（副詞片語）

958. The government_____ to approve the use of widespread surveillance strong
objections.
(A) is going
(B) had been

（C）was about

（D）can start

＜解答＞ C（動詞一致性）

959.　He insisted that John_____ it.

（A）do

（B）does

（C）did

（D）would do

＜解答＞ A（假設語氣）

960.　I don't take John's pen because I don't like_____.

（A）that pen of his

（B）that his pen

（C）his that pen

（D）that pen of him

＜解答＞ A（代名詞）

961.　I went to the dentist's yesterday, and I had two teeth_____.

（A）pulling

（B）to be pulled

（C）to be pulling

（D）pulled

＜解答＞ D（過去分詞）

962.　A yard was originally definded as the distance between the tip of the nose to the middle finger_____ of an English king.

（A）in the stretched out hand

（B）on the outreached hand

（C）on the stretching out hand

（D）at the outstretching hand

＜解答＞ B（形容詞片語）

963.　I didn't enjoy the concert yesterday; it was a confusion, and the band didn't play as it_____.

(A) did

(B) used to

(C) has done

(D) have done

<解答> B（副詞附屬子句）

964. According to many critics, much of Kolokoff's writing is_____.

(A) indistinct

(B) without distinction

(C) no distinction

(D) lack distinction

<解答> A（簡化）

965. Scientists continue to speculate_____ causes sunspots.

(A) for what

(B) what about

(C) whatever

(D) about what

<解答> D（名詞附屬子句）

966. Farmers rotate their crops_____ the soil will remain fertile.

(A) so that

(B) because of

(C) in order to

(D) rather than

<解答> A（連接詞形式）

967. Such problems_____ air and water pollution have no limited boundaries.

(A) like

(B) as

(C) of

(D) about

<解答> B（連接詞形式）

968. Violence on American campuses has abated_____.

（A）after 1970

（B）in 1970

（C）for1970

（D）since 1970

＜解答＞ D（介詞）

969. Most Americans don't object_____ them by their first mames.

（A）that I call

（B）to my calling

（C）for calling

（D）that I an call

＜解答＞ B（介詞）

970. General Grant had General Lee_____ him at Appomattox to sign the official surrender of the Confederate forces.

（A）to meet

（B）met

（C）meet

（D）meeting

＜解答＞ C（沒有 to 的不定詞）

971. _____ small specimen of the embryonic fluid is removed from a fetus, it will be possible to determine whether the baby will be born with birth defects.

（A）A

（B）That a

（C）If a

（D）When it is a

＜解答＞ C（條件句）

972. To generate income, magazine publishers must decide whether to increase the subscription price or_____.

（A）to see advertising

（B）if they should sell advertising

（C）selling advertising

（D）sold advertising

＜解答＞ A（連接詞的一致性）

973. _____ Java Man, who lived before the first Ice Age, is the first manlike animal.

（A）It is generally believed that

（B）Generally believed it is

（C）Believed generally is

（D）That it is generally believed

＜解答＞ A（主詞）

974. Prices for bikes can run_____$250.

（A）as high as

（B）as high to

（C）so high to

（D）so high as

＜解答＞ A（連接詞形式）

975. Travelers_____ their reservations well in advance if they want to fly during the Christmas holidays.

（A）had better to get

（B）had to get better

（C）had better get

（D）had better got

＜解答＞ C（副詞）

976. Flight nineteen from New York and Washington is now arriving at_____.

（A）gate two

（B）the gate two

（C）the two gate

（D）second gate

＜解答＞ A（名詞+基數）

977. The greater the demand, _____ the price.

（A）higher

（B）high

（C）the higher

（D）the high

　　＜解答＞ C（平行構句）

978. Benjamin West contributed a great deal to American art: _____.

（A）painting, teaching, and lecturing

（B）painting, as a teacher and lecturer

（C）painting, teaching, and as a lecturer

（D）painting, a teacher, and alecturer

　　＜解答＞ A（平行構句）

979. Upon hatching, _____.

（A）young ducks know how to swim

（B）swimming is known by young ducks

（C）the knowledge of swimming is in young ducks

（D）how to swim is known in young ducks

　　＜解答＞ A（主詞）

980. A seventeen-year-old is not_____ to vote in an election.

（A）old enough

（B）as old enough

（C）enough old

（D）enough old as

　　＜解答＞ A（字序）

981. After the assassination attempt, President Reagan's doctor suggested that he_____ a short rest at Camp David.

（A）will take

（B）would take

（C）take

（D）took

　　＜解答＞ C（假設語氣）

982. Not until a monkey is several years old_____ to exhibit signs of
independence from its mother.
（A）it begins
（B）does it begin
（C）and begin
（D）beginning
<解答> B（倒裝句）

983. Since Elizabeth Barrett Browning's never approved of_____ Robert
Browning, the couple doped to Italy where they lived and wrote.
（A）her to marry
（B）her marrying
（C）she marrying
（D）she to marry
<解答> B（代名詞形式）

984. Please write out the answers to the questions at the end of_____.
（A）eighth chapter
（B）eight chapter
（C）chapter eight
（D）chapter the eight
<解答> C（名詞+基數）

985. _____ to go to the grocery store every day ?
（A）Do people in your country like
（B）Won't people in your country like
（C）May people in your country like
（D）Have people in your country like
<解答> A（主詞和動詞的位置）

986. Although most adopted persons want the right to know who their natural
parents are, some who have found them wish that they_____ the experience of
meeting.
（A）hadn't

（B）didn't have had

（C）hadn't had

（D）hadn't have

＜解答＞　C（動詞時態）

987.　Kubrick's going to be nominated to receive the Academy award for best

director, _____?

（A）won't he

（B）didn't he

（C）doesn't he

（D）isn't he

＜解答＞　D（附加問題）

988.　The speaker is_____.

（A）very well acquainted with the subject

（B）recognized as an authority who knows a great deal in terms of the

subject

（C）someone who knows well enough about the subject which he has

undertaken to do the speaking

（D）a person who has close awareness of the subject that he speaks about so

much

＜解答＞　A（簡化）

989.　The Ford Theater where Lincoln was shot_____.

（A）must restore

（B）must be restoring

（C）must have been restored

（D）must restored

＜解答＞　C（被動語態）

990.　After seeing the movie Centennial, _____.

（A）the book was read by many people

（B）the book made many people want to read it

（C）many people wanted to read the book

（D）the reading of the book interested many people

＜解答＞ C（主詞）

991. The examiner made us＿＿＿＿ our identifications in order to be admitted to the test center.

（A）showing

（B）show

（C）showed

（D）to show

＜解答＞ B（沒有 to 的不定詞）

992. Doctoral students who are preparing to take their qualifying examinations have been studying in the library every night＿＿＿＿ the last three months.

（A）since

（B）until

（C）before

（D）for

＜解答＞ D（介詞）

993. ＿＿＿＿ of the play, Mourning Becomes Electra, introduces the cast of characters and hints at the plot.

（A）The act first

（B）Act one

（C）Act first

（D）First act

＜解答＞ B（名詞＋基數）

994. The Internal Revenue Service＿＿＿＿ their tax forms before April 15 every year.

（A）makes all Americans file

（B）makes all Americans to file

（C）makes the filing of all Americans

（D）makes all Americans filing

＜解答＞ A（沒有 to 的不定詞）

995. To answer accurately is more important than_____.

   （A）a quick finish

   （B）to finish qucikly

   （C）finishing quickly

   （D）you finish quickly

   ＜解答＞ B（比較）

996. A telephone recording tells callers_____.

   （A）what time the movie starts

   （B）what time starts the movie

   （C）what time does the movie start

   （D）the movie starts what time

   ＜解答＞ A（名詞附屬子句）

997. It costs about thirty dollars to have a tooth_____.

   （A）filling

   （B）to fill

   （C）filled

   （D）fill

   ＜解答＞ C（過去分詞）

998. Although Margaret Mead had several assistants during her long

   investigations of Samoa, the bulk of the research was done by_____ alone.

   （A）herself

   （B）she

   （C）her

   （D）hers

   ＜解答＞ C（代名詞形式）

999. Would you please_____ the listening comprehension script until after you

   have listened to the tape.

   （A）not to read

   （B）not read

   （C）don't read

（D）don't to read

＜解答＞ B（否定的祈使法語氣）

1000. When a body enters the earth's atmosphere, it travels_____.

（A）very rapidly

（B）in a rapid manner

（C）fastly

（D）with great speed

＜解答＞ A（副詞）

1001. Employers often require that candidates have not only a degree in engineering_____.

（A）but two years experience

（B）also two years experience

（C）but also two years experience

（D）but more two years experience

＜解答＞ C（連接詞形式）

1002. If one of the participants in a conversation wonders_____, no real communication has taken place.

（A）what said the other person

（B）what the other person said

（C）what did the other person say

（D）what was the other person saying

＜解答＞ B（字序）

1003. Professional people appreciate_____ when it is necessary to cancel an appointment.

（A）you to call them

（B）that you would call them

（C）your calling them

（D）that you are calling them

＜解答＞ C（主要子句）

1004. Farmers look forward to_____ every summer.

（A）participating in the county fairs

（B）participate in the county fairs

（C）be participating in the county fairs

（D）have participated in the county fairs

＜解答＞　A（動詞片語+動名詞）

1005.　Many embarrassing situations occur＿＿＿＿ a misunderstanding.

（A）for

（B）of

（C）because of

（D）because

＜解答＞　C（介詞片語）

1006.　＿＿＿＿ that gold was discovered at Sutter's Mill, and that the California Gold Rush began.

（A）Because in 1848

（B）That in 1848

（C）In 1848 that it was

（D）It was in 1848

＜解答＞　D（主詞）

1007.　Frost occurs in valleys and on low grounds＿＿＿＿ on adjacent hills.

（A）more frequently as

（B）as frequently than

（C）more frequently than

（D）frequently than

＜解答＞　C（比較）

1008.　It is important that the TOEFL Office＿＿＿＿ your registration.

（A）will confirm

（B）confirm

（C）confirms

（D）must confirm

＜解答＞　B（假設語氣）

1009. _____ that the English settled in Jamestown.

（A）In 1607 that it was

（B）That in 1607

（C）Because in 1607

（D）It was in 1607

＜解答＞ D（主詞）

1010. When friends insist on_____ expensive gifts, it makes most Americans
uncomfortable.

（A）them to accept

（B）their accepting

（C）they accepting

（D）they accept

＜解答＞ B（代名詞形式）

1011. As a safety measure, the detonator for a nuclear device may be made of_____
each of which is controlled by a different employee.

（A）two equipments

（B）two pieces of equipments

（C）two pieces of equipment

（D）two equipment pieces

＜解答＞ C（數量名詞+物質名詞）

1012. It is the first time that the Princess of Wales has been to the United States,
_____?

（A）isn't she

（B）hasn't she

（C）isn't it

（D）hasn't it

＜解答＞ C（附加問題）

1013. A child in the first grade tends to be_____ all of the other children in his
class.

（A）the same old to

（B）the same age than

（C）as old like

（D）the same age as

<解答> D（連接詞）

1014. We had hoped_____ the game, but the other team played very well.

（A）State University to win

（B）that State University win

（C）that State University would win

（D）State University's winning

<解答> C（名詞附屬子句）

1015. Unlike most Europeans many Americans_____ bacon and eggs for breakfast every day.

（A）used to eating

（B）are used to eat

（C）are used to eating

（D）used to eat

<解答> C（動詞片語+動名詞）

1016. Ancient civilizations such as the Phoenicians and the Mesopotamians_____ goods rather than use money.

（A）used to trade

（B）is used to trade

（C）used to trade

（D）was used to trade

<解答> C（動詞片語+不定詞）

1017. North Carolina is well known not only for the Great Smoky Mountains National Park_____ for the Cherokee Indian settlements.

（A）also

（B）and

（C）but also

（D）because of

<解答> C（連接詞形式）

1018. If a ruby is heated it_____ temporarily lose its color.

（A）would

（B）will

（C）does

（D）has

<解答> B（主要子句）

1019. All of the people at the AAME conference are_____.

（A）mathematic teachers

（B）mathematics teachers

（C）mathematics teacher

（D）mathematic's teachers

<解答> B（名詞當形容詞用）

1020. If it_____ more humid in the desert Southwest the hot temperatures would be unbearable.

（A）be

（B）is

（C）was

（D）were

<解答> D（假設語氣）

1021. For the investor who_____ money, silver or bonds are good options.

（A）has so little a

（B）has very little

（C）has so few

（D）has very few

<解答> B（形容詞附屬子句）

1022. According to the conditions of scholarship, after finishing my degree, _____.

（A）my education will be employed by the university

（B）employment will be given to me by the university

（C）the university will employ me

(D) I will be employed by the university

<解答> D（主要子句）

1023. _____ 1000 species of finch have been identified.

(A) As many as

(B) As many

(C) As much as

(D) Much as

<解答> A（連接詞）

1024. The United States is_____ that there are five time zones.

(A) much big

(B) too big

(C) so big

(D) very big

<解答> C（連接詞形式）

1025. Most insurance agents would rather you_____ anything about collecting claims until they investigate the situation.

(A) do

(B) didn't do

(C) don't

(D) didn't

<解答> B（動詞時態）

1026. The observation deck at the World Trade Center_____ in New York.

(A) is highest than any other one

(B) is higher than any other one

(C) is highest that any other one

(D) is higher that any other one

<解答> B（比較）

1027. _____ is necessary for the development of strong bones and teeth.

(A) It is calcium

(B) That calcium

（C）Calcium

（D）Although calicum

<解答> C（主詞）

1028. Only after food has been dried or canned_____.

（A）that it should be stored for later consumption

（B）should be stored for later consumption

（C）should it be stored for later consumption

（D）it should be stored for later consumption

<解答> C（倒裝句）

1029. Almost everyone fails_____ on the first try.

（A）in passing his driver's test

（B）to pass his driver's test

（C）to have passed his driver's test

（D）passing his driver's test

<解答> B（動詞片語）

1030. In many ways, riding a bicycle is similar to_____.

（A）the driving of a car

（B）when you drive a car

（C）driving a car

（D）when driving a car

<解答> C（平行構句）

1031. Canada does not require that U.S. citizens obtain passports to enter the country, and_____.

（A）Mexico does neither

（B）Mexico doesn't either

（C）neither Mexico does

（D）either does Mexico

<解答> B（縮減的子句）

1032. _____ the formation of the Sun, the planets, and other stars began with the condensation of an interslellar cloud.

  （A）It accepted that

  （B）Accepted that

  （C）It is accepted that

  （D）That is accepted

  ＜解答＞ C（主詞）

1033. The Consumer Price Index lists_____.

  （A）how much costs every car

  （B）how much does every car cost

  （C）how much every car costs

  （D）how much are every car cost

  ＜解答＞ C（字序）

1034. Fast-food restaurants have become popular because many working people want_____.

  （A）to eat quickly and cheaply

  （B）eating qucikly and cheaply

  （C）eat quickly and cheaply

  （D）the eat quickly and cheaply

  ＜解答＞ A（不定詞）

1035. _____, Carl Sandburg is also well known for his multivolume biography of Lincoln.

  （A）An eminent American poet

  （B）He is an eminent American poet

  （C）An eminent American poet who is

  （D）Despite an eminent American poet

  ＜解答＞ A（修飾的片語）

1036. Having been selected to represent the Association of American Engineers at the International Convention, _____.

  （A）the members applauded him

  （B）he gave a short acceptance speech

  （C）a speech had to be given by him

（D）the members congratulated him

＜解答＞ B（主詞）

1037. As soon as＿＿＿ with an acid, and sometimes water, is formed.

（A）a base will react

（B）a base reacts

（C）a base is reacting

（D）the reaction of a base

＜解答＞ B（主詞和動詞的一致）

1038. Although one of his ships succeeded in sailing all the way back to Spain through the Cap of Good Hope, Magellan never completed the first circumvention of the world, and＿＿＿.

（A）most of his crew didn't too

（B）neither most of his crew did

（C）neither did most of his crew

（D）most of his crew didn't also

＜解答＞ C（倒裝句）

1039. Weathering＿＿＿ the action whereby surface rock is disintegrated or decomposed.

（A）it is

（B）is that

（C）is

（D）being

＜解答＞ C（動詞）

1040. The people of Western Canada have been considering＿＿＿ themselves from the rest of the provinces.

（A）to separate

（B）separated

（C）separate

（D）separating

＜解答＞ D（動名詞）

1041. Not until a student has mastered algebra_____ the principles of geometry, trigonometry, and physics.

(A) he can begin to understand

(B) can he begin to understand

(C) he begins to understand

(D) begins to understand

<解答> B（倒裝句）

1042. Several of these washers and dryers are out of order and_____.

(A) need to be repairing

(B) repairing is required of them

(C) require that they be repaired

(D) need to be repaired

<解答> D（被動語態）

1043. Put plants_____ a window so that they will get enough light.

(A) near to

(B) near of

(C) next to

(D) nearly

<解答> C（副詞）

1044. Richard Nixon had been a lawyer and_____ before he entered politics.

(A) served in the Navy as an officer

(B) an officer in the Navy

(C) the Navy had him as an officer

(D) did service in the Navy as an officer

<解答> B（連接詞一致性）

1045. The salary of a bus driver is much higher_____.

(A) in comparison with the salary of a teacher

(B) than a teacher

(C) than that of teacher

(D) to compare as a teacher

<解答> C（比較）

1046. The assignment for Monday is to write a_____ about your hometown.

（A）fvie-hundred-word composition

（B）five-hundred-words composition.

（C）five-hundreds-words composition

（D）five-hundreds-word composition

<解答> A（名詞當形容詞用）

1047. A computer is usually chosen because of its simplicity of operation and ease of maintenance_____ its capacity to store information.

（A）the same as

（B）the same

（C）as well as

（D）as well

<解答> C（連接詞）

1048. Neptune is an extremely cold planet, and_____.

（A）so does Uranus

（B）so has Uranus

（C）so is Uranus

（D）Uranus so

<解答> C（倒裝句）

1049. The crime rate has continued to rise in American cities despite efforts on the part of both government and private citizens to curb_____.

（A）them

（B）him

（C）its

（D）it

<解答> D（代名詞一致性）

1050. As a safety precaution, all city cabdrivers carry only enough money to make change for a_____ bill.

（A）ten-dollar

（B）ten-dollars

（C）tens-dollar

（D）tens-dollars

＜解答＞ A（名詞當形容詞用）

1051. Staying in a hotel costs＿＿＿＿ renting a room in a dormitory for a week.

   （A）twice more than

   （B）twice as much as

   （C）as much twice as

   （D）as much as twice

   ＜解答＞ B（多重的比較）

1052. Gilbert Stuart is considered by most art critics＿＿＿＿ greatest portrait painter in the North American Clonies.

   （A）that he was

   （B）as he was

   （C）who was the

   （D）the

   ＜解答＞ D（比較）

1053. A student should tell a dorm counselor if＿＿＿＿ live with his roommate next year.

   （A）he'd rather not

   （B）he won't rather

   （C）he'll rather not

   （D）he'd rather didn't

   ＜解答＞ A（副詞附屬子句）

1054. ＿＿＿＿ two waves pass a given point simultaneously, they will have no effect on each other's subsequent motion.

   （A）So that

   （B）They are

   （C）That

   （D）If

＜解答＞ D（連接詞）

1055. Most foreign students don't like American coffee, and_____.

（A）I don't too

（B）either don't I

（C）neither don't I

（D）neither do I

＜解答＞ D（否定的一致性）

1056. This plant is_____ big that it should really be moved outside.

（A）so

（B）too

（C）such

（D）very

＜解答＞ A（連接詞）

1057. Among the astronomers for ancient Greece, two theories_____ concerning the place of the earth in the universe.

（A）developing

（B）in development

（C）developed

（D）which they developed

＜解答＞ C（動詞）

1058. The largest meteorite on display is in the American Museum in New York City, _____ over 34 tons.

（A）and it weighs

（B）it weighs

（C）its weight is

（D）which it weighs

＜解答＞ A（對等連接詞）

1059. There are several means_____ latitude and longitude.

（A）can determine

（B）to determine

（C）by them be determined

（D）we use them to determine

　　<解答>　B（修飾的不定詞片語）

1060.　The Homestead Act of 1862＿＿＿ to acquire land at a small cost.

（A）made possible

（B）made it possible

（C）made the possibility

（D）possibly made

　　<解答>　B（動詞+受詞+補語）

1061.　＿＿＿, Sir Issac Newton described the laws of gravitation.

（A）Was a seventeenth-century scientist

（B）Who was a seventeenth-century scientist

（C）A seventeenth-century scientist

（D）When was a seventeenth-century scientist

　　<解答>　C（修飾的片語）

1062.　Especially important to many people＿＿＿.

（A）there is legislation against pollution

（B）is legislation against pollution

（C）it is legislation against pollution

（D）legislation against pollution

　　<解答>　B（倒裝句）

1063.　Botanists are not sure where the first plant was grown or even＿＿＿.

（A）what plant was

（B）it was what plant

（C）what plant was it

（D）what plant it was

　　<解答>　D（名詞附屬子句）

1064.　If a star seems to be moving in a wavy line, ＿＿＿ of being a double star.

（A）we suspect

（B）that we suspect

（C）we suspect it

（D）the suspicion

＜解答＞ C（主要子句）

1065. The principle of a rocket motor is simple, _____ rockets are very complicated machines.

（A）large but which powerful

（B）but large, powerful

（C）large although powerful

（D）so large, powerful

＜解答＞ B（對等連接詞）

1066. _____ to find stars in pairs.

（A）It is very common

（B）Being very common

（C）Very common is

（D）That is very common

＜解答＞ A（虛假的主詞）

1067. James Cook, _____, also discovered the Hawaiian Islands.

（A）by exploring the South Sea he reached Australia

（B）expolred the South Sea and reaching Australia

（C）who explored the South Sea and reached Australia

（D）explored the South Sea then reached Australia

＜解答＞ C（形容詞附屬子句）

1068. One of the most obvious characteristics of the moon is the way in which it continuous changes_____.

（A）in appearing

（B）its appearance

（C）are appearing

（D）for appearance

＜解答＞ B（受詞）

1069. _____, John Glenn was a pioneer in the U.S. space program.

（A）Despite the first American who orbited the earth

（B）That the first American orbited the earth

（C）The first American to orbit the earth

（D）He was the first American to orbit the earth

＜解答＞ C（修飾的片語）

1070. Determining the mineral content of soil samples is an exacting process;

_____, experts must perform detailed tests the analyze soil specimens.

（A）so that

（B）however

（C）afterwards

（D）therefore

＜解答＞ D（連接詞）

1071. For the first time_____, large portions of the universe can be observed

simultaneously.

（A）since history

（B）in history

（C）history began

（D）of the beginning history

＜解答＞ B（修飾的片語）

1072. Early settlers needed trees, so they sent back to Europe for seedlings _____

around their houses.

（A）to plant

（B）and planted

（C）and plants

（D）which planted

＜解答＞ A（不定詞）

1073. Michael Faraday made a great discovery_____ that electricity can be made to

flow in a coil of wire.

（A）when he found

（B）to find

（C）was found

（D）be found

＜解答＞　A（副詞附屬子句）

1074. In 1939 the Ohio and Mississippi rivers overflowed＿＿＿ the worst flood ever known in the United States.

（A）the cause of

（B）which caused

（C）and caused

（D）they caused

＜解答＞　C（連接詞+複合動詞）

1075. Many craters on the earth's surface were probably by very large meteorites＿＿＿.

（A）smashing into the ground and exploding

（B）which smashed into the ground and an explosion

（C）when smashed into the ground was an explosion

（D）they smashed into the ground and exploded

＜解答＞　A（　修飾的片語）

1076. Throughout history, the moon has inspired not only song and dance＿＿＿.

（A）and also poetry and prose

（B）but poetry also prose

（C）together with poetry and prose

（D）but poetry and prose as well

＜解答＞　D（連接詞一致性）

1077. The earth might look like a perfect sphere, but careful measurements＿＿＿.

（A）show is not

（B）show that it is not

（C）that show it is not

（D）show it that is not

＜解答＞　B（動詞+名詞子句）

1078. Claudius Ptolemy, _____ of the first century A.D., left a good description of the geocentric theory.

（A）he was an astronomer and a philosopher

（B）being an astronomer and a philospher

（C）who was an astronomer and a philosopher

（D）an astronomer and who was a philosopher

＜解答＞ C（形容詞附屬子句）

1079. _____ coming the Space Age, a new dimension has been added to the study of the planets.

（A）While

（B）It is the

（C）When the

（D）With the

＜解答＞ D（導引片語）

1080. For many children, nothing seems so exciting_____ their first airplane ride.

（A）so does

（B）as

（C）on

（D）is

＜解答＞ B（連接詞）

1081. _____ a common belief, fright or excitement causes the flesh of young game fowel to turn a different color.

（A）It is a according to

（B）That it is according to

（C）While according to

（D）According to

＜解答＞ D（導引片語）

1082. Some bees make the characteristic monotonous noise known as buzzing_____.

（A）but their wings are vibrated rapidly

（B）the vibration of their wings is rapid

（C）by vibrating their wings rapidly

（D）and their wings rapidly vibrating

＜解答＞ C（修飾的片語）

1083. _____ pioneer days, a group of famers would bring together the livestock they wanted to sell so that one person could drive the animals to market.

（A）When

（B）It was during

（C）While

（D）In

＜解答＞ D（導引時間片語）

1084. _____ that modern corn may be a hybrid of teosinte and other wild species that no longer exist.

（A）Now is thought

（B）Thinking

（C）The thought

（D）It is thought

＜解答＞ D（虛假土詞）

1085. Only when humans employ nonchemical approaches to test control_____.

（A）will creatures such as roaches and rodents be successfully eliminated

（B）creatures such as roaches and rodents will be successfully eliminated

（C）if creatures such as roaches and rodents will be successfully eliminated

（D）that creatures such as roaches and rodents will be successfully eliminated

＜解答＞ A（倒裝句）

1086. In explaining the theory of relativity, the scientist states that mechanical laws which are true in one place_____ equally valid in any other place.

（A）being

（B）they should be

（C）are

（D）to be

＜解答＞ C（動詞一致性）

1087. Public transportation in most of the nation is expanding, _____, the use of subways and buses is declining in some metropolitan areas.

（A）Nevertheless

（B）Consequently

（C）Despite the fact

（D）Although

＜解答＞ A（對比連接詞）

1088. The Egytians and the Sumerians _____ copper as early as 5,000 years before Christ.

（A）they were using

（B）having used

（C）may have used

（D）using

＜解答＞ C（動詞過去式）

1089. Jupiter _____ perhaps the most important planet of the solar system.

（A）to be

（B）being

（C）is

（D）like

＜解答＞ C（動詞）

1090. _____, Thomas Edison invented adevice to transmit a special signal while he slept.

（A）He was a night telegraph operator

（B）That he was a night telegraph operator

（C）As a night telegraph operator

（D）Whereas a night telegraph operator

＜解答＞ C（導引片語）

1091. Training programs for the United States Peace Corps are conducted in the country or region_____ the volunteer will serve.

（A）and

（B）or

（C）but

（D）where

＜解答＞ D（附屬連接詞）

1092. _____ famous queens in the history of England: Elizabeth I and Victoria.

（A）Including two

（B）There are two

（C）For two

（D）Because are two

＜解答＞ B（虛假主詞）

1093. The Africa killer bees could not be handled safely, nor_____.

（A）could their honey be harvested

（B）their honey could be harvested

（C）harvested could their honey be

（D）could not their honey harvested

＜解答＞ A（疑問句字序）

1094. Playing a major role in the economic life of the United States, _____.

（A）women currently make 46 percent of the work force

（B）the women currently make up 46 percent of the work force

（C）women currently they make up 46 percent of the work force

（D）46 percent of the work force is currently made up of women

＜解答＞ A（主詞）

1095. Most psychologists agree that the basic structure of an individual's personality is_____.

（A）well established extremely by the age of five

（B）by the age of five it is extremely well established

（C）extremely well established by the age of five

（D）by the age of five and extremely well established

＜解答＞ C（字序）

1096. _____ Roman mythology, the god Jupiter was accepted as the most powerful ruler of the heavens.

（A）Like

（B）For

（C）With

（D）In

＜解答＞ D（介詞）

1097. An earthquake is a shaking of the ground_____ when masses of rock beneath the surface of the earth change position.

（A）which occurring

（B）it occurs

（C）and therefore occurring

（D）that occurs

＜解答＞ D（形容詞附屬子句）

1098. _____, authorities allow about one ton to each foot of length.

（A）To calculate the weight of an average adult whale

（B）They calculate the weight of an average adult whale

（C）In the calculation the weight of an average adult whale

（D）Even though they calculate the weight of an average adult whale

＜解答＞ A（導引子句）

1099. _____ the exception of insititutions controlled by church, municiapl, or private corporation, Latin American universities are regulated by federal laws.

（A）By

（B）For

（C）With

（D）To

＜解答＞ C（介詞）

1100. In Austria, where fertile farmland is limited, crops_____.
   （A）are on the sides of mountains often grown
   （B）often one on the sides of mountains grown
   （C）are grown on the sides often of mountains
   （D）are often grown on the sides of mountains
   ＜解答＞ D（動詞+字序）

1101. Racial violence erupted throughout the United States_____ Martin Luther
   King, Jr., was assassinated in April, 1968.
   （A）when
   （B）during
   （C）each time that
   （D）then
   ＜解答＞ A（時間副詞）

1102. _____ is called erosion.
   （A）The wearing away of land
   （B）When land wears away
   （C）Land which wears away
   （D）Wearing away land
   ＜解答＞ A（主詞）

1103. Firstborn children in a family seem to have a stronger desire to
   succeed_____.
   （A）than do later-born children
   （B）but later-born children do
   （C）as children born-later
   （D）if later-born children do
   ＜解答＞ A（比較）

1104. _____, we drove the horses into the stable.
   （A）Aware that a tornado was brewing
   （B）Because a tornado brewing
   （C）Although a tornado was brewing

（D）A tornado was brewing

＜解答＞　A（導引|片語）

1105. The geocentric idea was abandoned in the seventeenth century, partly as a result of the writings of Copernicus＿＿＿＿ observations made by other astronomers.

（A）and also were

（B）not only because of

（C）also because were

（D）and also because of

＜解答＞　D（對等連接詞）

1106. The universe＿＿＿＿ we know it might have begun with a great explosion.

（A）as

（B）that

（C）and which

（D）and

＜解答＞　A（狀態連接詞）

1107. Some areas of the moon are so full of craters＿＿＿＿ an extremely rough surface.

（A）that they present

（B）presenting

（C）which present

（D）to present

＜解答＞　A（形容詞附屬子句）

1108. Solid-fuel engines are simpler than liquid-fuel engines, ＿＿＿＿ have important uses.

（A）both of them

（B）so both

（C）both however

（D）but both

＜解答＞　D（對比連接詞）

1109. _____, Nethan Hale was a young schoolteacher living in Connecticut.

　　（A）When the American Revolution began

　　（B）The American Revolution began

　　（C）It was when the American Revolution began

　　（D）The begining of the American Revolution

　　＜解答＞ A（副詞附屬子句）

1110. The common garden pea, also called the English pea, _____ for its edible seeds.

　　（A）to grow

　　（B）is grown

　　（C）growing

　　（D）grow

　　＜解答＞ B（動詞）

1111. Nervous about flying in planes, _____.

　　（A）thirty years ago people knew nothing of space travel

　　（B）people knew nothing of space travel thirty years ago

　　（C）space travel was unknown by people thirty years ago

　　（D）because people knew nothing of space travel thirty years ago

　　＜解答＞ B（主詞）

1112. Rotation refers to the turning of the earth_____ to the movement around the sun.

　　（A）besides revolution

　　（B）revolution refers

　　（C）and revolution

　　（D）while revolution referring

　　＜解答＞ C（對等連接詞）

1113. The city's transport system, which is extremely old, _____ prove difficult to modernize.

　　（A）it might

　　（B）and might

（C）might

（D）that might

<解答> C（助動詞）

1114. _____, James Fenimore Cooper wrote about Indians and pioneers in the forest and sailors on the high seas.

（A）The first American novelist to ashieve world-wide fame who is

（B）The first American novelist to achieve world-wide fame

（C）Although he was the first American novelist to achieve worldiwide fame

（D）He was the first American novelist to achieve world-wide fame

<解答> B（名詞片語）

1115. Word of the first launchung of Sputnik I_____ the Observatory Philharmonic on October 4,1957.

（A）it reached

（B）was reached

（C）has been reaching

（D）reached

<解答> D（過去式）

1116. Pictures_____ with a telescope are inverted.

（A）taken

（B）they took them

（C）to take

（D）are taken

<解答> A（過去分詞當形容詞用）

1117. Bernard Foucault_____ in 1851 that the earth is rotating.

（A）who proved

（B）proved

（C）he proved

（D）it was proved

<解答> B（動詞）

1118. _____, but it also filters out harmful sun rays.

（A）The atmosphere gives us air to breathe

（B）Not only the atmosphere gives us air to breathe

（C）The atmosphere which gives us air to breathe

（D）Not only does the atmosphere give us air to breathe

＜解答＞ D（連接詞+倒裝句）

1119. Galileo's experiments with falling bodies, Pasteur's work disease germs,_____ on heredity are significant events in the story of science.

（A）also Mendel's research

（B）and Mendel's research

（C）and Mendel did research

（D）despite Mendel's research

＜解答＞ B（平行構句）

1120. Nicolaus Copernicus, _____, was born in Porum, Poland.

（A）is often considered the founder of modern astronomy

（B）whose founder of modernastronomy is often considered

（C）often considered the founder of modern astronomy

（D）who he is often considered the founder of modern astronomy

＜解答＞ C（修飾的片語）

1121. This vehicle bounces and glides along the ground_____.

（A）at an average speed of 40 miles per hour

（B）of 40 miles per hour at average speed

（C）at 40 miles per hour of an average speed

（D）of an average speed at 40 miles per hour

＜解答＞ A（副詞片語）

1122. _____, Harry S. Truman was our nation's thirty-third President.

（A）He was born and raised in Missouri

（B）Born and raised in Missouri

（C）Because he was born and raised in Missouri

（D）That he was born and raised in Missouri

<解答> B（導引片語）

1123. The earth revolves a little more rapidly_____ it is closer to the sun.

（A）when

（B）or

（C）than

（D）wherever

<解答> A（連接詞）

1124. The total influence of literature upon the course of human history_____.

（A）an evaluation is difficult

（B）is difficult to evaluate

（C）difficult to evaluate

（D）it is difficult to evaluate

<解答> B（動詞）

1125. The accomplishments of modern medicine would be possible_____ highly
specialized instruments.

（A）without

（B）but without

（C）but there are

（D）among

<解答> A（介詞）

1126. A planetarium is a special type of educational facility_____ the teaching of
astronomy.

（A）devoted to

（B）which devotes

（C）to devote

（D）to devote to

<解答> A（修飾的片語）

1127. _____, Charles Darwin did much to disprove common theories about
Biological evolution.

（A）He was a highly respected naturalist

（B）Because of he was a highly respected naturalist

（C）A highly respected naturalist

（D）A highly respected naturalist he was

＜解答＞ C（導引片語）

1128. ＿＿＿ pollution control measures are expensive, many industries hesitate to adopt them.

（A）Although

（B）However

（C）Because

（D）On account of

＜解答＞ C（連接詞）

1129. The moon is not a planet＿＿＿ the planets in many respects.

（A）resembling

（B）which resembles

（C）but resemblance to

（D）although it resembles

＜解答＞ D（形容詞附屬子句）

1130. ＿＿＿ with the size of the whole earth, the highest mountains do not seem high at all.

（A）When compared

（B）If you compare

（C）Compare them

（D）A comparison

＜解答＞ A（修飾的片語）

1131. Nebraska is a state whose name comes from an Indian word＿＿＿ " river in the flatness. "

（A）means

（B）the meaning

（C）meaning

（D）is meant

<解答> C（動名詞）

1132. Penguins usually do not get wet＿＿＿ their feathers are kept oily by tiny oil glands.

（A）so

（B）despite

（C）because

（D）yet

<解答> C（附屬連接詞）

1133. ＿＿＿ the first decade of the nineteenth century, the velocifere, the forerunner of the modern bicycle, lost favor temporaily.

（A）While

（B）It was

（C）During

（D）When

<解答> C（介詞）

1134. Francis Ford Coppola, who conceived, co-authored, and＿＿＿ God-father II, in one of America's most talented filmmakes.

（A）director of

（B）directed

（C）he directed

（D）directing

<解答> B（平行構句）

1135. ＿＿＿, the lion is a member of the cat family.

（A）Like the tiger

（B）Alike to the tiger

（C）Liking the tiger

（D）It is like the tiger

<解答> A（導引介詞片語）

1136. The amount of gravitational attraction between two objects depends on the mass of the objects and＿＿＿ between them.

（A）what is the distance

（B）the distance is

（C）the distance

（D）the distance what is

＜解答＞ C（受詞）

1137. Near the White House is another famous landmark_____ the Washington Monument.

（A）is which

（B）which call

（C）called

（D）it is called

＜解答＞ C（過去分詞）

1138. Marine reptiles are among the few creatures that are known to have a possible life span greater than_____.

（A）man

（B）the man's

（C）the one of man's

（D）that of man

＜解答＞ D（比較）

1139. A baby might show fear of an unfamiliar adult, _____ he is likly to smile and reach out to another infant.

（A）if

（B）whenever

（C）so that

（D）whereas

＜解答＞ D（對比連接詞）

1140. _____, they continue to overeat and eat the wrong foods.

（A）However many overweight people realize that they are threatening their health

（B）Many overweight people realizing that they are threatening their health

(C) Because of the fact that many overweight people realize that they are threatening their health

(D) Even though many overweight people realize that they are threatening their health

<解答> D（副詞附屬子句）

1141. As a congressman from Ohio, a Republican and_____ the antiwar movement, the young politician became well known during the 1960's.

(A) a leader of

(B) to lead

(C) leading

(D) he was leading

<解答> A（平行構句）

1142. _____ that it might be easier bo prepare a better map of the moon than of the earth.

(A) To say

(B) They say

(C) The saying

(D) It is said

<解答> D（虛假主詞）

1143. It is useful to science_____ the earth as an object in space.

(A) to consider

(B) which considers

(C) considers

(D) the consideration of

<解答> A（不定詞）

1144. _____ the financial means to remain in dependent, Thomas Edison was compelled to seek employment as a night telegraph operator.

(A) He was deprived of

(B) Deprived of

(C) That he was deprived of

（D）Although he was deprived of

＜解答＞ B（修飾的片語）

1145. One of the most beautiful natural wonders in the United States is the Grand
Canyon, _____ located in northwestern Arizona.

（A）and

（B）where

（C）is

（D）which is

＜解答＞ D（形容詞附屬子句）

1146. Although the gall bladeler is absent from all common members of the deer
family, _____.

（A）but the Asiatic musk deer has their organ

（B）this organ found in the Asiatic musk deer

（C）however this organ is found in the Asiatic musk deer

（D）this organ is found in the Asiatic musk deer

＜解答＞ D（主要子句）

1147. After the funeral, the residents of the apartment building_____.

（A）sent faithfully all weeks to the cemetery

（B）sent to the cemetery each week flowers faithfully

（C）sent flowers faithfully to the cemetery each week

（D）sent each week faithfully to the cemetery flowers

＜解答＞ C（動詞+字序）

1148. Captain Henry, _____, crept slowly through the underbrush.

（A）being remote from the enemy

（B）attempting to not encounter the enemy

（C）trying to avoid the enemy

（D）not involving himself in the enemy

＜解答＞ C（修飾的片語）

1149. The attorney told his client that_____.

（A）they had little chance of winning the case

（B）the case was of a small chance to win

（C）it was nearly impossible to win him the case

（D）the case had a minimum chance to be won by him

　　＜解答＞ A（名詞附屬子句）

1150. The cyclist_____ he crossed the main street.

（A）looked with caution after

（B）had looked cautiously before

（C）was looked cautious when

（D）look cautious when

　　＜解答＞ B（主要子句）

1151. I understand that the governor is considering a new proposal_____.

（A）what would elemate unnecessary writing in government

（B）who wants to cut down on the amount of writing in government

（C）that would elemate unnecessary paperwork in government

（D）to cause that the amount of papers written in government office will be reduced

　　＜解答＞ C（形容詞附屬子句）

1152. George did not do well in the class because_____.

（A）he studied bad

（B）he was not good studywise

（C）he was a badly student

（D）he failed to study properly

　　＜解答＞ D（副詞附屬子句）

1153. The committee has met and_____.

（A）they have reached a decision

（B）it has formulated themselves some opinions

（C）its decision was reached at

（D）it has reached a decision

　　＜解答＞ D（對等連接詞）

1154. _____, he began to make friends more easily.

（A）Having entered school in the new city, it was found that

（B）After entering the new school

（C）When he had been entering the new school

（D）Upon entering into the new school

＜解答＞ B（縮減的副詞子句）

1155. The bank sent a notice to its customers which contained_____.

（A）a remembrance that interest rates were to raise the following month

（B）a reminder that a raise in interest rates was the month following

（C）to remember that the interest rates were going up next month

（D）a reminder that the interest rates would rise the following month

＜解答＞ D（受詞+形容詞子句）

1156. The more she worked, _____.

（A）the less she achieved

（B）she achieved not enough

（C）she did not achieve enough

（D）she was achieving less

＜解答＞A（平行構句）

1157. John's score on the test is the highest in the class; _____.

（A）he should study last night

（B）he should have studied last night

（C）he must have studied last night

（D）he must had to study last night

＜解答＞ C（動詞過去式）

1158. The fact that space exploration has increased dramatically in the past thirty years_____.

（A）is an evidence of us wanting to know more of our sloar system

（B）indicates that we are very eager to learn all we can about our solar system

（C）how we want to learn more about the solar system

(D) is pointing to evidence of our intention to know a lot more about what is called our solar system

＜解答＞ B（動詞＋名詞子句）

1159. Jane changed her major from French to business_____.

(A) with hopes to be able easier to locate employment

(B) hoping she can easier get a job

(C) with the hope for being able to find better a job

(D) hoping to find a job more easily

＜解答＞ D（修飾的片語）

1160. Having been served lunch, _____.

(A) the problem was discussed by the members of the committee

(B) the committee members discussed the problem

(C) it was discussed by the committee members the problem

(D) a discussion of the problem was made by the members of the committee

＜解答＞ B（主詞）

1161. _____ received law degree as today.

(A) Never so many women have

(B) Never have so many women

(C) The women aren't ever

(D) Women who have never

＜解答＞ B（倒裝句）

1162. There were two small rooms in the beach house, _____ served as a kitchen.

(A) the smaller of which

(B) the smallest of which

(C) the smaller of them

(D) smallest of that

＜解答＞ A（比較）

1163. People all over the world are starving_____.

(A) greater in numbers

（B）in more numbers

（C）more numberously

（D）in great numbers

＜解答＞ D（形容詞片語）

1164. Manufacturers often sacrifice quality_____.

（A）for a larger profit margin

（B）in place of to earn more money

（C）to gain more quantities of money

（D）and instead earn a bigger amount of profit

＜解答＞ A（副詞片語）

1165. The professor said that_____.

（A）the students can turn over their reports on the Monday

（B）the reports on Monday could be received from the students by him

（C）the students could hand in their reports on Monday

（D）the students will on Monday the reports turn in

＜解答＞ C（名詞附屬子句）

1166. A major problem in the construction of new buildings_____.

（A）is that windows have been eliminated while air conditioning system have not been perfected

（B）is they have eliminated windows and still don't have good air conditioning

（C）is because windows are eliminated but air conditioners don't work good

（D）is dependent on the fact that while they have eliminated window, they are not capable to produce efficient air conditioning systems

＜解答＞ A（動詞+名詞子句）

1167. The manager angry because somebody_____.

（A）had allowed the photographers to enter the building

（B）had let the photographers to enter into the building

（C）permitting the photographers enter the building

　　（D）the photographers let into the building without the proper
　　　　documentations

　　＜解答＞ A（副詞附屬子句）

1168. The teachers have had some problems deciding_____.
　　（A）when to the students they shall return the final papers
　　（B）when are they going to return to the students the final papers
　　（C）when they should return the final papers to the students
　　（D）the time when the final papers they should return for the students

　　＜解答＞ C（副詞附屬子句）

1169. Fred's yearly income since he changed professions has_____.
　　（A）nearly tripled
　　（B）got almost three times bigger
　　（C）almost grown by three times
　　（D）just almost gone up three times

　　＜解答＞ A（簡化）

1170. The committee members resented_____.
　　（A）the president that he did not tell them about the meeting
　　（B）the president's not informing them of the meeting
　　（C）the president not to inform them of the meeting
　　（D）that the president had failed informing themselves that there was going
　　　　to be a meeting

　　＜解答＞ B（名詞片語）

1171. The rabbit scurried away in fright_____.
　　（A）when it heard the movement in the bushes
　　（B）the movement among the bushes having been heard
　　（C）after it was hearing moving inside of the bushes
　　（D）when he has heard that something moved in the bushes

　　＜解答＞ A（副詞附屬子句）

1172. The families were told to evacuate their houses immediately_____.
　　（A）at the time when the water began to go up

（B）when the water began to rise

（C）when up was going water

（D）in the time when the water raised

　　＜解答＞　B（副詞附屬子句）

1173. Tommy was one_____.

（A）of the happy childs of his class

（B）of the happiest child in the class

（C）child who was the happiest of all the class

（D）of the happiest children in the class

　　＜解答＞　D（比較）

1174. One of the professor's greatest attributes is_____.

（A）when he gives lectures

（B）how in the manner that he lectures

（C）the way to give lectures

（D）his ability lecture

　　＜解答＞　D（名詞片語）

1175. The doctor told his recepionist that he would return_____.

（A）as early as it would be possible

（B）at the earliest that it could be possible

（C）as soon as possible

（D）at the nearest early possibility

　　＜解答＞　C（連接詞）

1176. This university programs_____ those of Harvard.

（A）come second after

（B）are second only to

（C）are first except for

（D）are in second place from

　　＜解答＞　B（動詞）

1177. Alfred Adams has not_____.

（A）lived lonelynessly in times previous

（B）never before lived sole

（C）ever lived alone before

（D）before lived without the company of his friends

＜解答＞ C（避免雙重否定）

1178. ＿＿＿＿, the best car to buy is a Merceds Benz.

（A）Because of its durability and economy

（B）Because its lasts a long time, and it is very economical

（C）Because of its durability and it is economical

（D）Because durably and economize it is better than all the others

＜解答＞ A（導引片語）

1179. Henry will not be able attend the meeting tonight because＿＿＿＿.

（A）he must to teach a class

（B）he will be teaching a class

（C）of he wll teach a class

（D）he will have teaching a class

＜解答＞ B（副詞附屬子句）

1180. Many of the current international problems we are now facing＿＿＿＿.

（A）linguistic incompetencies

（B）are the result of misunderstandings

（C）are because of not understanding themselves

（D）lacks of the intelligent capabilities of understanding each other

＜解答＞ B（動詞的一致性）

1181. George would certainly have attended the proceedings＿＿＿＿.

（A）if he didn't get a flat tire

（B）if the flat tire hadn't happened

（C）had he not had a flat tire

（D）had the tire not flattened itself

＜解答＞ C（條件句）

1182. He has received several scholarships＿＿＿＿.

（A）not only because of his artistic but his academic ability

（B）for both his academic ability as well as his artistic

（C）because of his academic and artistic ability

（D）as resulting of his ability in the art and the academy

＜解答＞ C（副詞片語）

1183. He gave_____.

（A）to the class a tough assignment

（B）the class a tough assignment

（C）a tough assignment for the class

（D）an assignment very tough to the class

＜解答＞ B（受詞）

1184. Florida has not yet ratified the Equal Rights Amendment, and_____.

（A）several other states hasn't either

（B）neither has some of the others states

（C）some other states also have not either

（D）neither have several other states

＜解答＞ D（否定的一致性）

1185. Public television stations are different from commercial stations_____.

（A）because they receive money differently and different types of shows

（B）for money and program types

（C）in the areas of funding and programing

（D）because the former receives money and has programs differently from the latter

＜解答＞ C（修飾的片語）

1186. The students liked that professor's course because_____.

（A）there was few if any homework

（B）not a lot of homework

（C）of there wasn't a great amount of homework

（D）there was little or no homework

＜解答＞ D（主詞+形容詞）

1187. _____ that new information to anyone else but the sergeant.

（A）They asked him not to give

（B）They asked him to don't give

（C）They asked him no give

（D）They asked him to no give

＜解答＞ A（主詞+否定的不定詞）

1188. Automobile production in the United States_____.

（A）have taken slumps and rises in recent years

（B）has been rather evatic recently

（C）has been evatically lately

（D）are going up and down all the time

＜解答＞ B（動詞）

1189. _____ he would have come to class.

（A）If Mike is able to finish his homework

（B）Would Mike be able to finish his homework

（C）If Mike could finish his homework

（D）If Mike had been able to finish his homework

＜解答＞ D（條件句）

1190. _____, he would have been able to pass the exam.

（A）If he studied more

（B）If he were studying to a greater degree

（C）Studying more

（D）Had he studied more

＜解答＞ D（假設語氣）

1191. The doctor insisted that his patient_____.

（A）that he not work too hard for three months

（B）take it easy for three months

（C）taking it easy inside of three months

（D）to take some vacations for three months

＜解答＞ B（假設語氣）

1192. Ben would have studies medicine if he_____ to a medical school.

（A）could be able to enter

（B）had been admitted

（C）was admitted

（D）were admitted

＜解答＞ B（條件句）

1193. This year will be difficult for this organization because_____.

（A）they have less money and volunteers than they had last year

（B）it has less money and fewer voluteers than it had last year

（C）the last year it did not have as few and little volunteers and money

（D）there are fewer money and volunteers that in the last year there

＜解答＞ B（主詞+形容詞）

1194. John said that no other car could go_____.

（A）os fast like his car

（B）as fast like his car

（C）as fast like the car of his

（D）as fast as his car

＜解答＞ D（連接詞形式）

1195. The facilities of the older hospital_____.

（A）is as good or better than the new hospital

（B）are as good or better that the new hospital

（C）are as good or better than the new hospital

（D）are as good as or better than those of the new hospital

＜解答＞ D（連接詞+比較）

1196. Richard was asked to withdraw from graduate school because_____.

（A）they believed he was not really able to complete research

（B）he was deemed incapable of completing his research

（C）it was decided that he was not capable to complete the research

（D）his ability to finish the research was not believed or trusted

＜解答＞ B（主詞）

1197. She wanted to serve some coffee to her guests; however, _____.

（A）she hadn't many sugar

（B）there was not a great amount of the sugar

（C）she did not have much sugar

（D）she was lacking in amount of the sugar

＜解答＞ C（主詞+形容詞）

1198. While attempting to reach his home before the storm, _____.

（A）the bicycle of John broke down

（B）it happened that John's bike broke down

（C）the storm caught John

（D）John had an accident on his bicycle

＜解答＞ D（主詞）

1199. The teacher suggested that her students_____ experiences with ESP.

（A）write a composition on their

（B）to write composition about the

（C）wrote some compositions of his or her

（D）had written any compositions for his

＜解答＞ A（假設語氣）

1200. _____ did Arthur realize that there was danger.

（A）Upon entering the store

（B）When he entered the store

（C）After he entered the store

（D）Only after entering the store

＜解答＞ D（倒裝句）

1201. Todd_____ the science assignment.

（A）understands

（B）understand

（C）understanding

（D）will understood

＜解答＞ A（動詞）

1202. The Petrified Forest_____ for amateur hikes.

（A）is not

（B）is not recommended

（C）not

（D）recommended

＜解答＞ B（動詞被動式）

1203. She_____ him a magic golden bridle.

（A）give quickly

（B）to give quick

（C）quickly gave

（D）quick gave

＜解答＞ C（副詞）

1204. You might need a calculator_____.

（A）until that problem

（B）by that problem

（C）above that problem

（D）for that problem

＜解答＞ D（介詞）

1205. The first Indenpendence Day celebration was a time_____.

（A）Monday

（B）raining day

（C）nice holiday

（D）for bonfires and noise

＜解答＞ D（形容詞片語）

1206. A small cardboard pilgrim stands_____.

（A）beautiful

（B）too good

（C）beside each plate

（D）very good

＜解答＞ C（副詞片語）

1207. The hotel manager gave my_____ directions

(A) aunt and I

(B) aunt and me

(C) aunt and we

(D) they and we

＜解答＞ B（間接受詞）

1208. The residents of the mainland_____ roe a delicacy.

(A) consider

(B) considers

(C) considering

(D) have considered

＜解答＞ A（主詞和動詞一致性）

1209. How many sixth-graders have never_____.

(A) ridden on the school bus

(B) rode on the school bus

(C) ride on the school bus

(D) rides on the school bus

＜解答＞ A（動詞時態）

1210. Instead of hugging, _____ so hard they could not say the lines correctly.

(A) them laughed

(B) they laughed

(C) there laugh

(D) their laugh

＜解答＞ B（易混淆的字）

1211. _____, but the patient had already recovered.

(A) The doctor has come

(B) The doctor immediately

(C) The doctor came immediately

(D) The doctor come

＜解答＞ C（副詞片語）

1212. The ship has just completed a voage_____.

（A）today's weather

（B）good weather

（C）weather

（D）through rough weather

＜解答＞ D（介詞片語）

1213. I hope I improve my grades, _____ this term.

（A）I have gone

（B）I studied

（C）I have studied

（D）for I have been studying hard

＜解答＞ D（連接詞）

1214. Most club members voted in favor of the hayride, but_____.

（A）voted it

（B）voted against it

（C）many voted against it

（D）many against it

＜解答＞ C（代名詞子句）

1215. Heather, who is new at our school, is_____ I know.

（A）her

（B）the nicest girl

（C）the nicer girl

（D）she

＜解答＞ B（述語主格）

1216. Nobody wanted to read the book, _____.

（A）a thick hardback with a fadded cover

（B）too old and difficult

（C）is beautiful

（D）it is interesting

＜解答＞ A（同位語）

1217. In America, citizens have the right _____.

  （A）to speak their minds

  （B）speaking their minds

  （C）that speak their minds

  （D）they speak their minds

  ＜解答＞ A（不定詞片語）

1218. People sit late_____ drinking tropical fruit juices and chatting.

  （A）very happy

  （B）into the night

  （C）today's party

  （D）is a good party

  ＜解答＞ B（副詞片語）

1219. _____, the movie has not yet come to our local theaters.

  （A）Releasing

  （B）Recent releasing

  （C）Recently released

  （D）Has released

  ＜解答＞ C（過去分詞）

1220. The colonel will be commending the scout for_____ for the dangerous mission.

  （A）volunteer

  （B）volunteered

  （C）has volunteered

  （D）volunteering

  ＜解答＞ D（現在分詞）

1221. The man was given a ticket for_____.

  （A）driving the wrong way on a one-way street

  （B）drives the wrong way on a one-way street

  （C）to drive the wrong way on a one-way street

  （D）drived the wrong way on a one-way street

  ＜解答＞ A（分詞片語）

1222. _____ early morning good for anything but sleeping.

  （A）I would used to consider

  （B）I however used to consider

  （C）I am used to consider

  （D）I never used to consider

  ＜解答＞ D（副詞）

1223. Farmers used the plentiful lobsters as fertilizer_____ their gardens.

  （A）by

  （B）for

  （C）about

  （D）with

  ＜解答＞ B（介詞）

1224. Father rented a truck, _____, and we had to make several trips.

  （A）it is large enough

  （B）but it was large enough

  （C）but it wasn't large enough

  （D）it wasn't large enough

  ＜解答＞ C（連接詞）

1225. Under her management as corporation president, _____ sold millions of

  carpet sweepers.

  （A）that

  （B）who

  （C）the company

  （D）their

  ＜解答＞ C（主詞）

1226. In that drawer must be her_____.

  （A）herself

  （B）them

  （C）a lot of

  （D）scissors and letter opener

<解答> D（複合主詞）

1227. This library contained a large_____ of ancient plays and works of philosophy.

    （A）collection

    （B）working

    （C）beautiful

    （D）amount

    <解答> A（直接受詞）

1228. Three figures are painted_____; they represent Past, Present, and Future.

    （A）on the ceiling

    （B）finished

    （C）red and purple

    （D）big area

    <解答> A（副詞片語）

1229. _____ the defense attorney made her final plea, the prisoner sat stiffly in a chair.

    （A）Although

    （B）So that

    （C）As

    （D）If

    <解答> C（附屬連接詞）

1230. _____, the moon rose, and navigation became less difficult.

    （A）In darkness for two hours after flying

    （B）After flying in darkness for two hours

    （C）After they had been flying in darkness for two hours

    （D）For two hours in darkness after they had been flying

    <解答> C（搖擺的修飾）

1231. One of the guides asked Sean and_____ boys wanted to operate the computer.

    （A）I if us

    （B）me if we

    （C）me if us

（D）I if we

＜解答＞ B（代名詞）

1232. After someone told her it looked_____ her name with a y instead of an i.

（A）less affected she spelled

（B）less affected; she spelled

（C）less affected: she spelled

（D）less affected, she spelled

＜解答＞ D（標點符號）

1233. The cost of living is rising, for_____ for gassoline and other products.

（A）consumer's prices

（B）consumbers

（C）consumbers' prices

（D）consumers must pay higher prices

＜解答＞ D（獨立子句）

1234. She shouldn't_____ all by herself when she could have joined our car poll.

（A）of driven

（B）have driven

（C）off driven

（D）has driven

＜解答＞ B（易混淆的字）

1235. We didn't want to take the boat out because the_____.

（A）waves looked rather choppy

（B）waves looked sort of choopy

（C）waves looked more choppy

（D）waves looked much choppy

＜解答＞ A（易混淆的字）

1236. In our English class_____.

（A）that Prearl buck wrote The Good Earth we learned that

（B）we learned that Prearl Buck wrote The Good Earth

（C）The Good Earth we learned that Prearl Buck wrote

（D）We wrote The Good Earth we learned that Prearl Buck

＜解答＞　B（字序）

1237.　I dived off the high board_____ the pool.

　　（A）swim the length of

　　（B）have swan the length of

　　（C）swam the length of

　　（D）swun the length of

　　＜解答＞　C（動詞時態）

1238.　Seeing a car with an out-of-state license plate in my driveway, I ran inside, and_____?

　　（A）whom do you think was there

　　（B）who do you think was there

　　（C）whoever do you think was there

　　（D）whomever do you think was there

　　＜解答＞　B（代名詞）

1239.　Could it be that nobody among all the world's animal lovers_____?

　　（A）wants to take these puppies off my hands

　　（B）want to take these puppies off my hands

　　（C）to want to take these puppies off my hands

　　（D）have wanted to take these puppies off my hands

　　＜解答＞　A（主詞和動詞一致性）

1240.　The happiest time in my life was_____.

　　（A）a nice holiday

　　（B）swimming summer

　　（C）to go to library

　　（D）when we went to Colombia for the summer

　　＜解答＞　D（名詞子句）

1241.　English is a_____ is similar to that of many Scandinavian languages.

　　（A）Germanic language, its structure

　　（B）Germanic language. Its structure

（C）Germanic language its structure

（D）Germanic language: its structure

＜解答＞ B（連續句子）

1242. When you haven't got enough iodine in your blood, _____.

（A）you get a garner

（B）you get a garter

（C）you get a goiter

（D）you get a goldbeater

＜解答＞ C（易混淆的字）

1243. _____ to the Civil War as the War Between the States.

（A）This history book refers

（B）In this history book they refer

（C）This history book it refers

（D）In this history book it refers

＜解答＞ A（代名詞）

1244. To finish her paper on time, _____

（A）Mary's weekend was spent in the library

（B）Mary spent her weekend in the library

（C）so that Mary spent her weekend in the library

（D）that Mary spent her weekend in the library

＜解答＞ B（搖擺的修飾）

1245. After the celebration we were introduced to the president and_____.

（A）master of ceremonies

（B）master

（C）to the master of ceremonies

（D）ceremonies

＜解答＞ C（清晰的修飾）

1246. The wrong spelling_____ the true origin of the word and gives the false impression that its source is contemporary English.

（A）hiding

（B）has hided

（C）hided

（D）hides

＜解答＞　D（動詞）

1247. The offices＿＿＿＿.

（A）have been designed for high efficiency

（B）designed for high efficiency

（C）have designed

（D）for high efficiency

＜解答＞　A（句子）

1248. ＿＿＿＿, the sailors rejoiced as they arrived on time.

（A）It is warm weather and clear skies

（B）To be by warm weather and clear skies

（C）Having been aided by warm weather and clear skies

（D）That was aided by warm weather and clear skies

＜解答＞　C（現在分詞片語）

1249. Many countries have festivals in March＿＿＿＿ can be traced back to ancient celebrations of spring.

（A）he

（B）one

（C）that

（D）it

＜解答＞　C（關係代名詞）

1250. How many of us posses the skills＿＿＿＿ on our own without the assistance of store-bought items？

（A）having survived

（B）to survive

（C）will have survived

（D）to have survived

＜解答＞　B（動詞時態）

1251. _____ the Tsang family had installed a smoke detector in their home, their lives were saved.

（A）Because

（B）Because of

（C）That

（D）Where

＜解答＞ A（附屬連接詞）

1252. At the end of the game, _____.

（A）the coach nor the team members could account for lopsided score

（B）neither the coach nor the team members could account for the lopsided score

（C）neither the coach and the team members could account for the lopsided score

（D）and the coach nor the team members could account for the lopsided score

＜解答＞ B（對等連接詞）

1253. _____ had grown into a cat that small but glossy and beautiful.

（A）Having found a good home the scrawny undernourished kitten

（B）Having found a good home, the scrawny undernourished kitten

（C）Having found a good home, the scrawny, undernourished kitten

（D）Having found a good home the scrawny, undernourished kitten

＜解答＞ C（標點符號）

1254. The manager insisted that there wasn't_____ reason for making the customers wait so long.

（A）none

（B）not

（C）no

（D）any

＜解答＞ D（易混淆的字）

1255. We were grateful to our knowledgeable_____ us patiently throughout the year.

　　（A）coach has guided

　　（B）coach guided

　　（C）coach and who guided

　　（D）coach, who guided

　　＜解答＞ D（標點符號）

1256. _____, the band's melody line was drowned out.

　　（A）Because the drummer play worse

　　（B）Because the drummer play worst

　　（C）Because the drummer play badly

　　（D）Beacuse the drummer play bad

　　＜解答＞ C（副詞）

1257. As soon as we returned to the campsite, _____.

　　（A）we discovered that someone took our food and gear

　　（B）we discovered that someone had taken our food and gear

　　（C）we discovered that someone had been taken our food and gear

　　（D）we had discovered that someone had taken our food and gear

　　＜解答＞ B（假設語氣）

1258. Mrs. Ames was pleased that when_____, he passed easily.

　　（A）her son took the driver's test

　　（B）the driver's test was taken by her son

　　（C）took the driver's test her son

　　（D）by her son took the driver's test

　　＜解答＞ A（笨拙的動詞）

1259. _____, I'm sure we would not be stranded on the highway now.

　　（A）If we would have had the engine tuned

　　（B）If we have had the engine tuned

　　（C）If we were the engine tuned

　　（D）If we will have had the engine tuned

<解答>　A（假設語氣）

1260. _____ a short-answer test in history instead of an essay exam.

（A）Were hoping to have had

（B）Were hoping to have

（C）Were hoping to have been had

（D）Were hoping to be have been

<解答>　B（不定詞時態）

1261. At a party, _____ are the best noisemakers.

（A）a band

（B）the big

（C）balloons or horns

（D）this drum

<解答>　C（複合主詞）

1262. My brother_____ a bike instead.

（A）for a watch but

（B）but a bike

（C）asked for a watch but received

（D）asked for a watch but

<解答>　D（複合動詞）

1263. The dentist or his assistant_____ my teeth every six months.

（A）clean and polish

（B）cleans and polish

（C）clean and polishes

（D）cleans and polishes

<解答>　D（複合主詞+複合動詞）

1264. Many people think that_____ is the greastest pilot in America.

（A）general chuck Yeager

（B）General chuck Yeager

（C）General Chuck Yeager

（D）general chuck yeager

<解答> C（專有名詞大寫）

1265. Dad told the mechanics to call＿＿＿ know how much his bill would be.
    （A）him to let him
    （B）him to let he
    （C）he to let him
    （D）he to let he

<解答> A（代名詞）

1266. I watched until the sky was＿＿＿ stars.
    （A）bright with twinkling
    （B）brightly and twinklingly
    （C）bright with twinkle
    （D）brighted and twinkled

<解答> A（形容詞）

1267. At age twenty-one the squire usually＿＿＿ ready for knighthood.
    （A）made
    （B）kept
    （C）appeared
    （D）pushed

<解答> C（連繫動詞）

1268. The pictures won't be developed＿＿＿ Friday or Saturday.
    （A）either
    （B）until
    （C）among
    （D）between

<解答> B（介詞）

1269. Have you read the book＿＿＿?
    （A）that the teen-age werewolf
    （B）about the teen-age werewolf
    （C）the teen-age werewolf
    （D）of the teen-age werewolf

<解答> B（介詞片語當形容詞）

1270. Several paintings by that artist_____ on exhibit at the mall.

（A）is

（B）were

（C）are

（D）was

<解答> C（主詞和動詞一致性）

1271. Under the starry sky, the campers were_____ in their sleeping bags.

（A）lie

（B）lay

（C）laying

（D）lying

<解答> D（易混淆的字家族）

1272. The black moths could be_____ frequently killed by birds.

（A）easily seen they were

（B）easily seen. They were

（C）easily seen, they were

（D）easily seen-they were

<解答> B（連續句子）

1273. Fridays and other days always_____ longer than regular school days.

（A）seemed

（B）seeming

（C）seems

（D）seem

<解答> D（主詞和動詞一致性）

1274. _____ was a great success.

（A）The first performance of the play

（B）The play

（C）The performance

（D）The performance and the play

<解答> A（完整句子）

1275. Somebody said that there would be no more＿＿ movie tickets.
（A）discountingly
（B）discounted
（C）discounting
（D）discount
<解答> C（名詞當形容詞用）

1276. Several people in the audience showed by＿＿ enthusiasm that they had enjoyed watching the matches.
（A）them
（B）themselves
（C）their
（D）their's
<解答> C（代名詞所有格）

1277. During the press conference the＿＿ commented on the congressional vote.
（A）President's
（B）president
（C）President
（D）presidents
<解答> C（專有名詞大寫）

1278. The baby across the street owns a＿＿ clock that has ivory numbers.
（A）Swiss
（B）swiss
（C）Swiss'
（D）swiss'
<解答> A（專有名詞當形容詞）

1279. The balance of nature quite＿＿ depends on all kinds of animals even on the ones that are not cute and cuddly.
（A）definites
（B）definitely

（C）definite

（D）definiting

＜解答＞ B（副詞）

1280. The girls' basketball team not only_____ the most points in our school's history.

（A）won the game and scored

（B）won the game but scored

（C）won the game because scored

（D）won the game but also scored

＜解答＞ D（連接詞）

1281. How did the well-prepared student_____ answer the examination questions？

（A）genially

（B）ungraciously

（C）reverently

（D）comprehensively

＜解答＞ D（使用正確的字）

1282. How did the nervous patient _____ approach the dentist's chair？

（A）barbarously

（B）ferociously

（C）reluctantly

（D）nocturnally

＜解答＞ C（使用正確的字）

1283. If someone falls from a boat, throw a life vest or another_____ object.

（A）float

（B）qualified

（C）buoyant

（D）cautious

＜解答＞ C（使用正確的字）

1284. Kill whales_____ can be trained to perform trick.

（A）（that's what Shamu）

（B）that's what Shamu

（C）thats-what-Shamu

（D）that's what, Shamu

　　<解答> A（標點符號）

1285. My sister＿＿＿ say that the new teacher is a favorite of their's.

（A）Janets

（B）Janet's

（C）Janet

（D）Janet's being

　　<解答> B（表示所有）

1286. ＿＿＿ turn is it to summariz the President's speech?

（A）Who's

（B）Whose

（C）Who is

（D）Who has

　　<解答> B（易混淆的字家族）

1287. The＿＿＿ promised to appoint a committee to correct the problem.

（A）mayor, a member of the audience, soon

（B）mayor a member of the audience soon

（C）mayor, a member of the audience soon

（D）mayor a member of the audience, soon

　　<解答> A（標點符號）

1288. If I had started my report sooner, ＿＿＿.

（A）I have finished it on time

（B）I finished it on time

（C）I had finished it on time

（D）I might have finished it on time

　　<解答> D（條件句）

1289. The boiler＿＿＿, but fortunately no one was in the basement at the time.

（A）burst

（B）busted

（C）burton

（D）bursar

　　＜解答＞　A（易混淆的字）

1290. I this morning's paper, ＿＿＿＿.

（A）I read about the bank robbers who were captured

（B）who were captured I read about the bank

（C）I read about the bank who were captured

（D）about the bank who were captured I read

　　＜解答＞　A（錯位修飾）

1291. That novel takes in the＿＿＿＿ and highlights the problems of the feudal system.

（A）middle ages

（B）Middle Ages

（C）Middle Age

（D）middle's ages

　　＜解答＞　B（專有名詞大寫）

1292. Our gym teacher to us today to do all the exercises＿＿＿＿.

（A）slows

（B）slow

（C）slowly

（D）slowed

　　＜解答＞　C（副詞）

1293. After she became blind, ＿＿＿＿ than anyone else.

（A）she claims she has better sight

（B）she was claiming she had better sight

（C）she was claimed she had better sight

（D）she claimed she had better sight

　　＜解答＞　D（肯定語態）

1294. We watched another canoeist and saw how_____ could barely steer our canoe.

   （A）her

   （B）herself

   （C）her's

   （D）she

   ＜解答＞　D（代名詞主格）

1295. An argument broke out between Mr. Morales and_____ over the location of the property lines.

   （A）they

   （B）them

   （C）themselves

   （D）their

   ＜解答＞　B（代名詞受格）

1296. To apply for the scholarship, a student must submit at least four samples of_____ work.

   （A）one's

   （B）my

   （C）his or her

   （D）their

   ＜解答＞　C（主詞和代名詞一致性）

1297. _____ on the bus is supposed to stay in his seat.

   （A）Everybody

   （B）They

   （C）Somebody

   （D）We

   ＜解答＞　A（前置詞和代名詞一致性）

1298. Everybody in the chorus_____.

   （A）are trying out for the play

   （B）is trying out for the play

（C）were trying out for the play

（D）have been trying out for the play

＜解答＞ B（主詞和動詞一致性）

1299. Sailors, _____, were hired to string the miles of cable.

（A）working a great heights

（B）who used to work heights

（C）who to work a great heights

（D）who were used to working a great heights

＜解答＞ D（附屬子句）

1300. In one corner we stacked a mound of debris_____.

（A）so that it could be hauled away

（B）so it could be hauled away

（C）that it could be hauled away

（D）it could be hauled away

＜解答＞ A（副詞＋附屬連接詞）

1301. If you are interested in _____, give me a call after school and let me know.

（A）to the concert tonight

（B）attending the concert tonight

（C）attended the concert tonight

（D）have attended the concert tonight

＜解答＞ B（動名詞片語）

1302. _____ people have become concerned about proper eating habits.

（A）In the last few decades

（B）From the last few decades

（C）About the last few decades

（D）By the last few decades

＜解答＞ A（介詞片語當副詞）

1303. I did not have time _____ the football game on television.

（A）watch

（B）to watch

（C）to watching

（D）watching

＜解答＞ B（不定詞當形容詞）

1304. The Nineteenth of the Constitution_____ in 1920, was largely the result of Catt's efforts.

（A）adopts

（B）to adopt

（C）adopted

（D）adopting

＜解答＞ C（過去分詞）

1305. Some of my friends earn extra money_____.

（A）is baby sitting

（B）that baby-sitting

（C）about baby-sitting

（D）by baby-sitting

＜解答＞ D（分詞當介詞的受詞）

1306. The governor has done everything possible_____.

（A）retaining the present tax structure

（B）retained the present tax structure

（C）to retain the present tax structure

（D）has retained the present tax structure

＜解答＞ C（介詞片語）

1307. He felt increasingly_____ with the actions of his friends.

（A）is unhappy

（B）to be unhappy

（C）unhappy

（D）unhappyly

＜解答＞ C（述語形容詞）

1308. _____ with enjoyment for nearly two hundred years.

（A）This classic

（B）This classic has been read

（C）This classic reads

（D）This classic is reading

　　＜解答＞　B（主詞+動詞片語）

1309. _____, it put many workers out of work, and this has been the case with most technological advances.

（A）Although this was good for the manufacturers

（B）This was good for the manufacturers

（C）By this was good for the manufacturers

（D）With this was good for the manufacturers

　　＜解答＞　A（連接詞）

1310. The teacher told the students " Take your essays_____ for revision and hand them to me tomorrow. "

（A）go to home

（B）going home

（C）home

（D）to be home

　　＜解答＞　C（名詞當副詞用）

1311. The reason for the windespread concern for eagles_____ many are dying from lead poisoning.

（A）is because

（B）is that

（C）is which

（D）is where

　　＜解答＞　B（連接詞）

1312. _____ had lived in Montreal for five years, she could speak both French and English.

（A）Being as

（B）Because

（C）Being that

（D）Because of

＜解答＞ B（連接詞）

1313. Whenever I'm not going＿＿＿ challenging, I grow bored easily.

（A）something

（B）nothing

（C）anything

（D）some

＜解答＞ A（易混淆的字）

1314. The picture on this television set is＿＿＿ than on that one.

（A）much clearer

（B）much more clearer

（C）much clearer the

（D）much clearest

＜解答＞ A（雙重比較）

1315. In each graduating class, the valedictorian is the student whose average is higher than that of＿＿＿.

（A）any senior

（B）some senior

（C）some other senior

（D）any other senior

＜解答＞ D（比較要清楚）

1316. The weather this afternoon is＿＿＿ than it was this morning.

（A）pleasanter

（B）much pleasant

（C）pleasantly

（D）more pleasant

＜解答＞ D（比較級）

1317. After the first act, we all applauded＿＿＿.

（A）enthusiastic

（B）enthusiastically

（C）more enthusiastic

（D）much more enthusiastic

　　＜解答＞ B（副詞）

1318. Williams insisted that every employee_____ to the company picnic.

　　（A）is invited

　　（B）be invited

　　（C）was invited

　　（D）is being invited

　　＜解答＞ B（假設語氣）

1319. " I wish_____ next year already so that I would be in College, " John said.

　　（A）were

　　（B）was

　　（C）had

　　（D）would

　　＜解答＞ A（假設語氣）

1320. 　　　 by the crowds and praised by the press.

　　（A）The space travelers were cheered

　　（B）The space travelers cheered

　　（C）The space travelers are cheered

　　（D）The space travelers have cheered

　　＜解答＞ A（被動語態）

1321. The rescue squad_____ their ladder to get her down.

　　（A）arrived they used

　　（B）arrived, they used

　　（C）arrived. They used

　　（D）arrived. they used

　　＜解答＞ C（連續句子）

1322. Saturday we and our parents_____.

　　（A）to the lake and swam

　　（B）drove to the lake and swam

(C) the lake and swam to drove

(D) drove and swam to the lake

＜解答＞ B（複合動詞）

1323. _____ before playing soccer with us.

(A) She made her homework

(B) She did she homework

(C) She did his homework

(D) She did her homework

＜解答＞ D（代名詞）

1324. Some of the_____ objects require special temperture and humidity control.

(A) value

(B) valued

(C) valuably

(D) valuable

＜解答＞ D（形容詞）

1325. The judge_____.

(A) has scary in her costume

(B) got scary in her costume

(C) looked scary in her costume

(D) will scary in her costume

＜解答＞ C（連繫動詞）

1326. Did Nancy finish her report, _____.

(A) or is she still working on it

(B) of is she still working on it

(C) and is she still working on it

(D) that is she still working on it

＜解答＞ A（連接詞）

1327. Neither the tomatoes nor the peach_____ ripe.

(A) were

(B) was

（C）are

（D）is

＜解答＞ D（主詞和動詞一致性）

1328. The experience_____ other sense as important as sight.

（A）does

（B）makes

（C）do

（D）make

＜解答＞ B（主詞和動詞一致性）

1329. All warmed up again, _____.

（A）I have sink into sleep

（B）I got sink into sleep

（C）I sank into a deep sleep

（D）I sink into a deep sleep

＜解答＞ C（動詞時態）

1330. My little brother_____ still for only a few seconds at a time.

（A）set

（B）has sit

（C）have set

（D）sits

＜解答＞ D（易混淆的字）

1331. Many citizens of the United States still use the old system_____ and corporations have switched to the metric system.

（A）of measurment, but many professions

（B）of measurment many professions

（C）of measurment and many professions

（D）of measurment; many professions

＜解答＞ A（連續的句子）

1332. For many years the diary_____ in a secret shorthand.

（A）had been written

（B）had

（C）had written

（D）wrote

＜解答＞ A（動詞片語被動式）

1333. _____ and studied the map of the mountain trails.

（A）The hikers load their backpacks

（B）The hikers loaded their backpacks

（C）The hikers loading their backpacks

（D）The hikers to load their backpacks

＜解答＞ B（複合動詞）

1334. This parakeet screeches if you don't give him_____ seed.

（A）to

（B）enough

（C）for

（D）already

＜解答＞ B（形容詞）

1335. Casals played a strong game that she seemed to be rewarding us for_____ support.

（A）us

（B）we

（C）our

（D）ourselves

＜解答＞ C（代名詞所有格）

1336. The new exchanges student who comes from Noway is_____.

（A）surprising fluent in English

（B）fluently surprisingly in English

（C）fluent surprisingly in English

（D）surprisingly fluent in English

＜解答＞ D（副詞）

1337. _____, this one has remained among the best known.

（A）Out of hundreds of legends

（B）Hundreds of legends

（C）Hundreds of legends out of

（D）Out of legends of hundreds

＜解答＞ A（介詞片語）

1338. I didn't receive a letter from my cousin today, _____.

（A）nor did I really expect one

（B）I really nor did expect one

（C）I really did nor expect one

（D）nor I did really expect one

＜解答＞ A（倒裝句）

1339. The principal was excited, _____.

（A）for the school board had approved his plan for a new cafeteria

（B）the school board had approved his plan for a new cafeteria

（C）about the school board had approved his plan for a new cafeteria

（D）nice the school board had approved his plan for a new cafeteria

＜解答＞ B（字序+連接詞）

1340. While the mountain lion looked around for food, _____.

（A）the fawn perfectly remained still

（B）remained perfectly still the fawn

（C）the fawn remained perfectly still

（D）perfectly still the lion remained

＜解答＞ C（述語形容詞）

1341. Does this_____ brief description of Plato's state lead you to accept or reject his ideas of government ?

（A）more

（B）quitely

（C）quite

（D）much

＜解答＞ C（副詞）

1342. Women receive an education＿＿＿ equal to men and fight alongside men in wars with neighboring states.
（A）exactly
（B）exact
（C）most exact
（D）how exactly
＜解答＞ A（副詞）

1343. William knew she'd have＿＿＿ to witness the eclipse.
（A）to get up incredible early
（B）to get up incredibly early
（C）to get up early incredibly
（D）to get up incredibly earlier
＜解答＞ B（副詞修飾副詞）

1344. ＿＿＿, but Father's mind was made up.
（A）Neither my mother nor I was enthusiastic
（B）Either my mother or I was enthusiastic
（C）Neither my mother and I was enthusiastic
（D）Neither my mother for I was enthusiastic
＜解答＞ B（連接詞）

1345. ＿＿＿ failed to latch onto the special pin on the satellite.
（A）The front docking adapter on of his spacesuit
（B）A docking of his spacesuit adapter on the front of
（C）A docking adapter on the front of his spacesuit
（D）The front of his spacesuit a docking adapter on
＜解答＞ C（完整主詞+字序）

1346. The whole town mourned＿＿＿.
（A）the early death
（B）its most famous son
（C）the early death of its most famous son
（D）its most famous the early

＜解答＞ C（完整述語+動詞）

1347. The newborn calf rose its feet with a wobbling motion and_____.

（A）stood for the first time

（B）stands for the first time

（C）for the first time

（D）for the first time to stand

＜解答＞ A（複合動詞）

1348. _____, she was planning to go on with her training.

（A）Accepting the coach's advice

（B）Accepted the coach's advice

（C）The coach's advice was accepted

（D）Advice was accepted the coach's

＜解答＞ A（分詞片語）

1349. We watch the dancers_____.

（A）being practice

（B）having practiced

（C）practiced

（D）practice the new routine

＜解答＞ D（沒有 to 的不定詞）

1350. The members, _____, have varied interests.

（A）in fact

（B）people from all walks of life

（C）on the other hand

（D）according to

＜解答＞ B（同位片語）

1351. You_____ can be a good speller if you really have the desire.

（A）tool

（B）to

（C）two

（D）too

<解答> D（易混淆的字）

1352. If you see the_____ in the hall, tell him he is wanted in the main office.

　　（A）princess

　　（B）principal

　　（C）principle

　　（D）principicum

　　<解答> B（易混淆的字）

1353. Jack's achievenent test scores ranked_____.

　　（A）in the eighty-eighth percentile

　　（B）in the eighty eighth precentile

　　（C）in the eighty, eighth percentile

　　（D）in the eighty; eighth percentile

　　<解答> A（標點符號）

1354. The club members celebrated_____.

　　（A）Bastille day by having dinner at a French restaurant

　　（B）bastille day by having dinner at a French restaurant

　　（C）Bastille Day by having dinner at a French restaurant

　　（D）bastille day by having dinner at a french restaurant

　　<解答> C（專有名詞大寫）

1355. Let us work a while longer on the motor; _____.

　　（A）we can't hardly leave it this way

　　（B）we hardly leave it this way

　　（C）we never hardly leave it this way

　　（D）we don't hardly leave it this way

　　<解答> B（雙重否定）

1356. _____, there are fewer mosquitoes this summer.

　　（A）Since there scarcely any rain last spring

　　（B）Since there wasn't scarcely any rain last spring

　　（C）Since there never wasn't any rain last spring

　　（D）Since there wasn't not any rain last spring

<解答> A（雙重否定）

1357. Looking through the telescope, _____.

（A）seemed enormous I thought the moon

（B）I seemed enormous the moon thought

（C）I thought the moon seemed enormous

（D）the moon seemed enormous I thought

<解答> C（搖擺的修飾）

1358. _____, the floor got scratched.

（A）Doing a few tap dance steps

（B）While I was doing a few tap dance steps

（C）While a few tap dance steps I was doing

（D）Doing a few tap while I was

<解答> B（搖擺的修飾）

1359. _____, but it was actually ahead of schedule.

（A）The train is seemed slowly

（B）The train has seemed slow

（C）The train seemed slow

（D）The train seemed slowly

<解答> C（形容詞）

1360. My sister_____ into my room to remind me to clean up the mess in the kitchen.

（A）came

（B）come

（C）coming

（D）comed

<解答> A（動詞時態）

1361. After three long years of wearing braces, I_____ pleased with the results.

（A）couldn't help but feel

（B）couldn't help feeling

（C）couldn't help to feel

（D）couldn't help but feeling

＜解答＞ B（易混淆的字）

1362. _____, the flames had already begun to spread.

（A）By the time we smelled the smoke

（B）By the time we had smelled the smoke

（C）By the time we was smelled the smoke

（D）By the time we smelling the smoke

＜解答＞ A（動詞時態）

1363. _____, she was considered the most popular teacher in the school.

（A）Even though her standards will be high

（B）Even though her stands is high

（C）Even though her standards were high

（D）Even though her standards would be high

＜解答＞ C（條件句）

1364. He would have second the winning basket_____.

（A）if he would have kept his eye on the clock

（B）if he had kept his eye on the clock

（C）if he kept his eye on the clock

（D）if he had been kept his eye on the clock

＜解答＞ B（假設語氣）

1365. The missing painting_____ to the museum.

（A）returned

（B）returning

（C）to return

（D）has been returned

＜解答＞ D（動詞被動語態）

1366. After metal had been discovered, _____.

（A）these earlier implements were being used by later people as models

（B）these earlier implements were used by later people as models

（C）these earlier implements are used by later people as models

（D）these earlier implements used by later people as models

＜解答＞ B（假設語氣）

1367. When you change the battery in the car, _____ your eyes and hands from the sulfuric acid in the battery.

（A）to have been protected

（B）to be protected

（C）to have protected

（D）to protect

＜解答＞ D（動詞時態）

1368. The title of salutatorian goes to_____ has the second highest academic average.

（A）whoever

（B）whomever

（C）who

（D）whose

＜解答＞ A（代名詞）

1369. Do you have time to show Larry and_____ how to change the oil？

（A）us

（B）we

（C）our

（D）ourselves

＜解答＞ A（代名詞受格）

1370. The answer that people_____ is that they never wear out because needles never touch them.

（A）who like them gave

（B）who like them give

（C）who like them gives

（D）who like them giving

＜解答＞ B（前置詞和動詞一致）

1371. On my way to school I always walk_____ the bakery.

（A）paste

（B）passed

（C）past

（D）passive

＜解答＞　C（易混淆的字）

1372. There candidates have filed for the_____them have any previous experience in public office.

（A）new commission seat-none of

（B）new commission seat: none of

（C）new commission seat; none of

（D）new commission seat, none of

＜解答＞　C（標點符號）

1373. The reason you are tired is_____ we watched the late show.

（A）because

（B）that

（C）so that

（D）which

＜解答＞　B（連接詞）

1374. According to my friend Juan, Houston, Texas, is more interesting and more exciting than_____ in that state.

（A）city

（B）a city

（C）any city

（D）any other city

＜解答＞　D（比較時自己要除外）

1375. _____, I'd have been glad to help them paint the house.

（A）If they haven't too proud to ask

（B）If they aren't too proud to ask

（C）If they weren't too proud to ask

（D）If they hadn't been too proud to ask

<解答> D（假設語氣）

1376. When their parents_____ shopping, the twins decided to play some computer games.

（A）had gone

（B）had went

（C）have gone

（D）went

<解答> A（動詞時態）

1377. It's funny how even an assistant supervisor can make her meaning clear to people like_____ in just a few sentences.

（A）him

（B）himself

（C）us

（D）ourselves

<解答> C（代名詞）

1378. None of the competitors knew what_____ own chances of winning were.

（A）her

（B）its

（C）his

（D）their

<解答> D（代名詞和前置詞一致）

1379. However, _____ had been offered of the link between exercise and fitness.

（A）until recently no scientific proof

（B）until recently no scientific prooves

（C）until recently no scientific

（D）until recently no

<解答> A（主詞）

1380. One of the passengers told the bus driver_____ the route very well.

（A）that she didn't know

（B）that the driver didn't know

（C）that anyone didn't know

（D）that I didn't know

＜解答＞　B（模糊的代名詞）

國家圖書館出版品預行編目資料

TOEFL 托福文法與構句／李英松著. — 初版. —
[新北市]：李昭儀, 2023.07
　　冊；　公分
ISBN 978-626-01-1240-0 (上冊：平裝)

1.CST: 托福考試 2.CST: 語法

805.1894　　　　　　　　　112005959

TOEFL托福文法與構句 上冊

作　　者　李英松

發 行 人　李英松

出　　版　李昭儀
　　　　　Email：lambtyger@gmail.com

設計編印　白象文化事業有限公司
　　　　　專案主編：李婕　　經紀人：徐錦淳

經銷代理　白象文化事業有限公司
　　　　　412台中市大里區科技路1號8樓之2（台中軟體園區）
　　　　　出版專線：（04）2496-5995　　傳真：（04）2496-9901
　　　　　401台中市東區和平街228巷44號（經銷部）
　　　　　購書專線：（04）2220-8589　　傳真：（04）2220-8505

印　　刷　普羅文化股份有限公司

初版一刷　2023 年 7 月

定　　價　420 元

白象文化　印書小舖 PressStore　出版・經銷・宣傳・設計
www·ElephantWhite·com·tw　f 自費出版的領導者　購書 白象文化生活館